THE INFINITE ADVENTURES OF SUPERNOVA

PEPPER PAGE

SAVES THE UNIVERSE!

THE INFINITE ADVENTURES OF SUPERNOVA

PEPPER PAGE

SAVES THE UNIVERSE!

Story by

Landry Q. Walker
and Eric Jones

Script: Landry Q. Walker
Art: Eric Jones
Colors: Eric Jones, Michael "Rusty" Drake,
Pannel Vaughn
Letters: Patrick Brosseau
Producer: Jon Guhl

New York

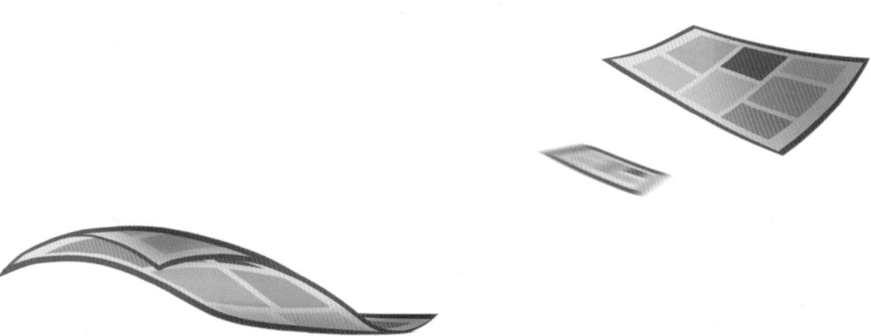

STERLING CITY.
THE HEART OF THE CIVILIZED WORLD.

FOR LONG IT STOOD AS A SYMBOL OF PROSPERITY AND PEACE.

AND THEN, IN ONE QUICK FLASH OF LIGHT...

...EVERYTHING CHANGED.

AND FROM THIS DOORWAY, THEY EMERGED--MONSTERS FROM BEYOND...THINGS THAT COULD NOT BE NAMED...

THE SUPERVILLAINS HAD ARRIVED.
AND IN THEIR WAKE...
...ALL WOULD SUFFER.

BUT HOPE WAS NOT YET LOST.
FOR CHAOS MUST ALWAYS BE BALANCED. AND SO...
...THE OVERLORDS OF ORDER SENT THEIR OWN CREATION--A BEING OF PERFECTION SWORN TO PROTECT THIS WORLD.
A CHAMPION OF TRUTH, INTEGRITY, AND THE RIGHTS OF ALL.
A HERO.
AND HER NAME WOULD BE REMEMBERED FOREVER.
SUPERNOVA! HERO FROM THE FUTURE!
WHERE DID SHE COME FROM?!
WHAT ARE HER MAGNIFICENT POWERS?!
DISCOVER ALL THE EXCITING ANSWERS IN EACH MONTH'S HISTORY-SHATTERING ISSUE!

OMIGOSH!
THE OVERLORDS OF ORDER SENT THEIR OWN CREATION—A BEING OF PERFECTION SWORN TO PROTECT THIS WORLD.
A HERO.
A CHAMPION OF TRUTH, INTEGRITY, AND THE RIGHTS OF ALL.
AND HER NAME WOULD BE REMEMBERED FOREVER.
SUPERNOVA!
HERO FROM THE FUTURE!
WHAT ARE HER MAGNIFICENT POWERS?!
DISCOVER ALL THE EXCITING ANSWERS IN EACH MONTH'S HISTORY-SHATTERING ISSUE!

I CAN'T BELIEVE I GOT THE WHOLE BOX FOR ONLY TWENTY CRED-UNITS!
I MEAN...YOU READ ON SCREENS AND IT SEEMS SO VIVID. BUT THEN YOU GET THE REAL PRINTED COMICS... IT'S LIKE GOING **BACK IN TIME!**
AND THE DIALOGUE! SO DIFFERENT AFTER THE GOLDEN AGE **REBOOT!**

"BAH! YOU'RE TOO LATE TO STOP ME, **SUPER-NOVA!** THE **STARFORCE** IS ALMOST MINE...
"AND WITH IT... THE GATEWAY TO ETERNITY **WILL BE OPENED!"**

"NO, **MENDAX...** NO MORE OF THIS.
"YOU CAN'T TAKE **THIS** POWER.

"BECAUSE IT'S **NOT** JUST THE STAR-FORCE...

"...IT'S ***ME."***

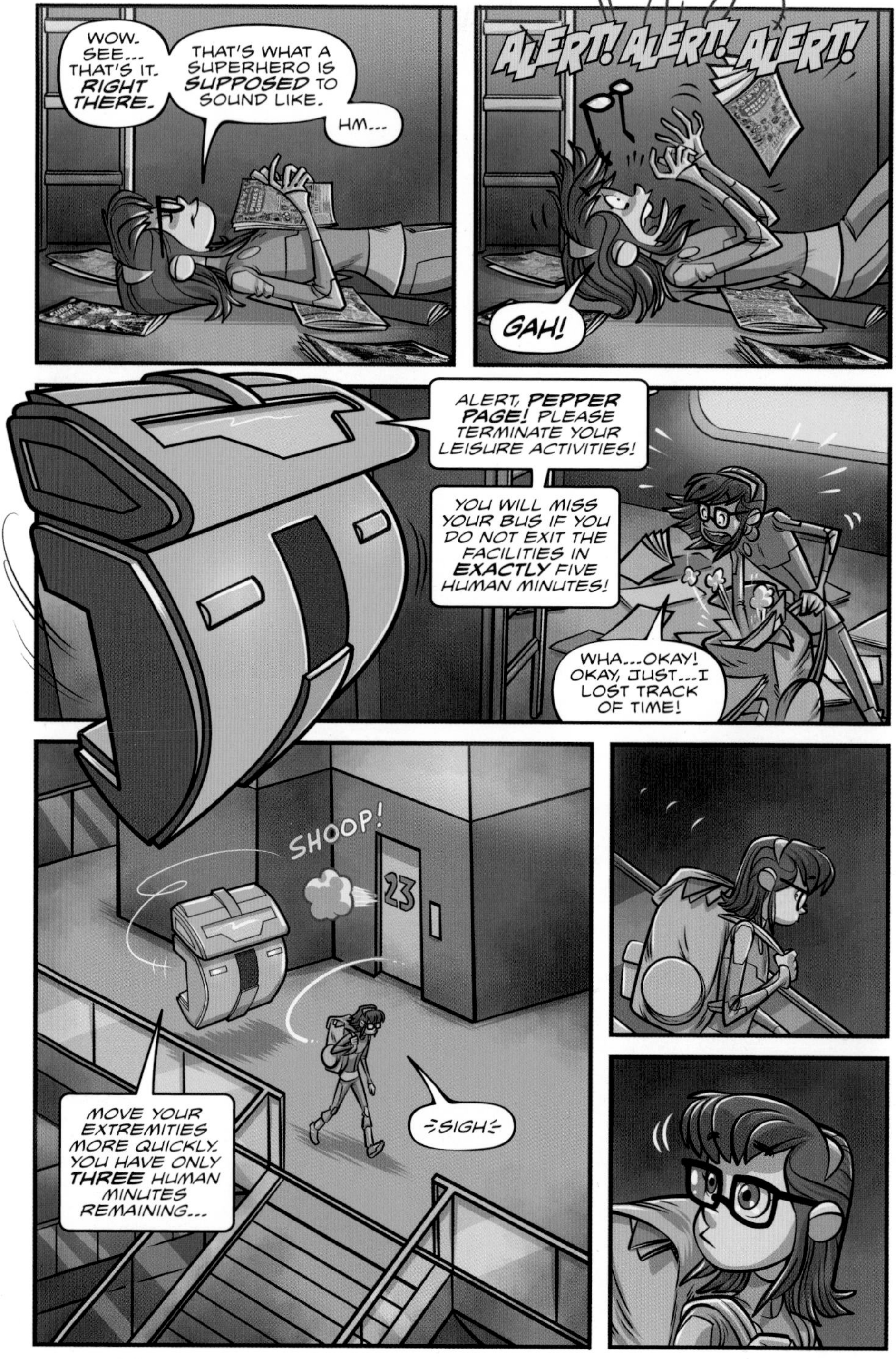

ALERT, **PEPPER PAGE!** PLEASE TERMINATE YOUR LEISURE ACTIVITIES!

YOU WILL MISS YOUR BUS IF YOU DO NOT EXIT THE FACILITIES IN **EXACTLY** FIVE HUMAN MINUTES!

WHA...OKAY! OKAY, JUST...I LOST TRACK OF TIME!

SHOOP!

23

MOVE YOUR EXTREMITIES MORE QUICKLY. YOU HAVE ONLY **THREE** HUMAN MINUTES REMAINING...

-SIGH-

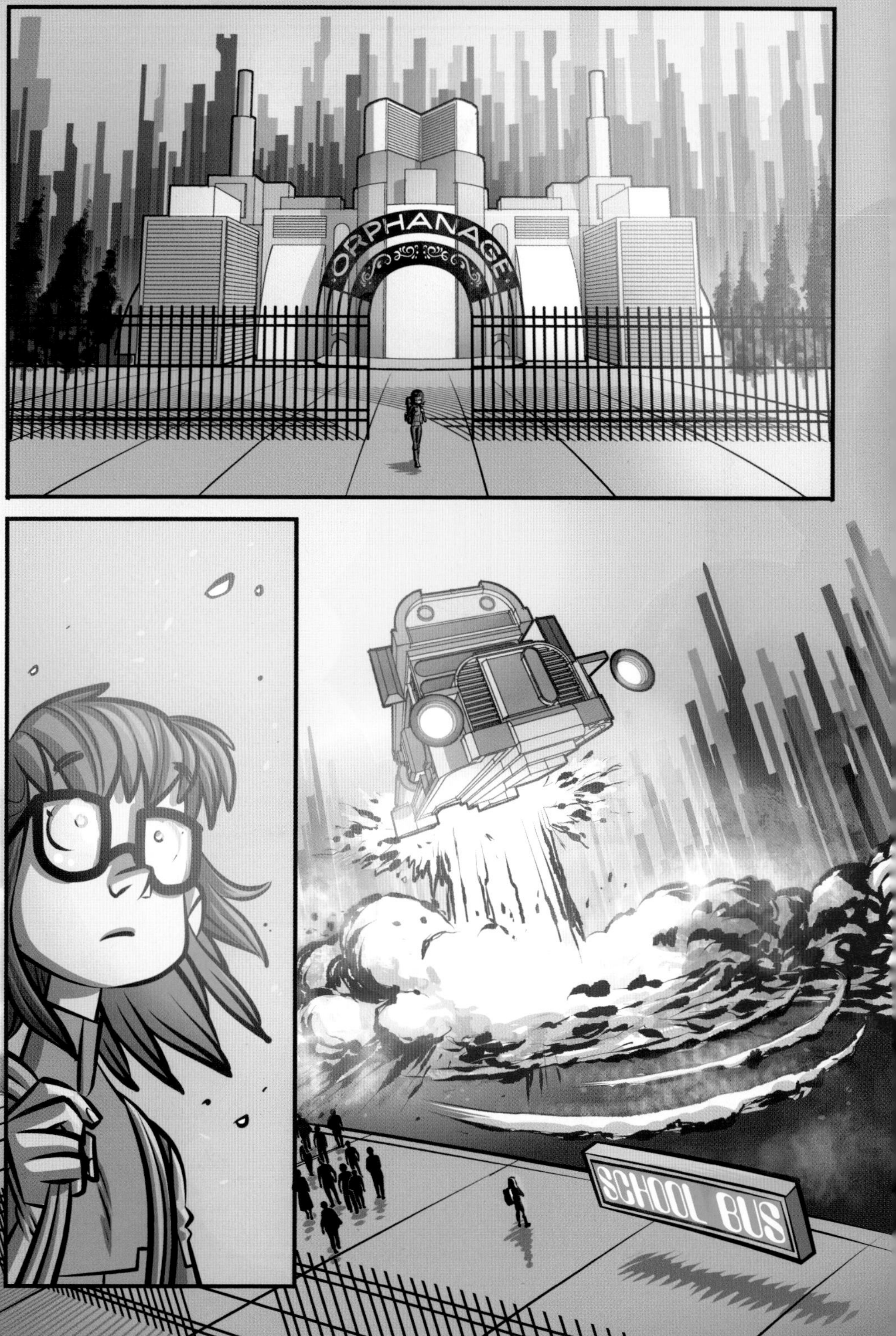

ORPHANAGE
SCHOOL BUS

SUPERNOVA MET **GRIMDARK THE DREAD DETECTIVE** BEFORE THEY JOINED THE **DANGER CLUB?** OH, RIGHT... THEY REWROTE THAT WHEN CHRONOS ERASED THE **TIMELINE...**
500 ARMY MEN

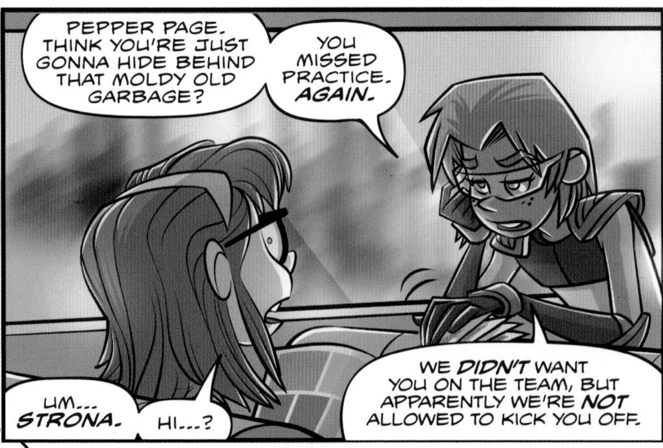
PEPPER PAGE. THINK YOU'RE JUST GONNA HIDE BEHIND THAT MOLDY OLD GARBAGE?
YOU MISSED PRACTICE. **AGAIN.**
UM... **STRONA.**
HI...?
WE **DIDN'T** WANT YOU ON THE TEAM, BUT APPARENTLY WE'RE **NOT** ALLOWED TO KICK YOU OFF.

SEE... I DON'T KNOW IF YOU NOTICED, BUT OUR TEAM IS **0 FOR 8.** AND YOU KNOW **WHY?**
BECAUSE WE'RE **TERRIBLE?**
BECAUSE **YOU'RE** TERRIBLE. YOU DRAG THE WHOLE TEAM **DOWN.** BUT WE NEED A THIRD-STOP OR WE GET **DISQUALIFIED!**

WON'T MISS THE GAME. I **REALLY** WON'T.
THAT'S WHAT YOU **ALWAYS** SAY!
HEY!
YOU'RE GONNA WRINKLE THAT! IT'S A **COLLECTIBLE!**

SERIOUSLY? **THIS** IS WHAT YOU WASTE TIME ON INSTEAD OF PRACTICE?

JUST GIVE IT **BACK!**
"NIGHT FALLS WHEN **ECLIPSA** STRIKES!"
PFF! WAS THIS WRITTEN BY **BABIES?**

THIS IS OUR LAST CHANCE TO MAKE THE PLAYOFFS! DO YOU KNOW WHAT HAPPENS IF WE LOSE THIS GAME?
NO. BECAUSE I NEVER WANTED TO PLAY BUT THE CLASS WAS RANDOMLY ASSIGNED TO ME AND I HAVE NO CHOICE...
UGH! YOU'RE LIKE...SO IRRITATING! MAYBE SPORTS DON'T MATTER TO YOU, BUT THEY MATTER TO EVERYONE ELSE!
YOU STUPID ORPHAN! YOU COST ME THIS WIN AND I'LL--
SPLAT!
AH.
AHH!
AGHHH!
OH NO! MY SANDWICH! IT STRANGELY SLIPPED FROM MY HANDS AND HURLED ITSELF AT STRONA'S FACE!
GRR...
I'M JUST SO SORRY TO INTERRUPT YOUR INSULTING AND DEMEANING TIRADE!
GIVE PEPPER HER COMIC BACK, STRONA. LEAVE HER ALONE. I'M SERIOUS.

STRONA SALANN.
I'M STREAMING YOUR BULLY-FEST TO MY HOME CHANNEL. IT'S SET TO AUTO-TAG YOUR PARENTS IN A MINUTE. SO MAYBE JUST...WALK AWAY AND I'LL SHUT IT DOWN?
OR FACE THE WRATH OF THIS BANANA. FOR REAL, I JUST SAID THAT.

PAH! WHATEVER, TALLY. DO YOU THINK I CARE IF MY PARENTS SEE YOUR STUPID LIVESTREAM? I'M LOOKING OUT FOR MY TEAM!

YOU HEAR THAT? YOUR FRIEND IS TOO AFRAID TO EVEN TRY.

YOU BETTER NOT COST US ANY MORE GAMES, PAGE. I'M WARNING YOU.
CAREFUL!

KEEP WALKING...I'M STILL STREAMING THIS...
BAH.

GOT IT.

HEY... YOU REALLY BOUGHT THE ORIGINALS? PAPER ALWAYS FEELS SO WEIRD TO TOUCH...

"MENDAX... YOU FIEND! WHAT HAVE YOU DONE TO THE EARTH?!"
ZOLA...

THAT'S EXACTLY THE KIND OF STUFF STRONA WAS TEASING ME ABOUT!
GRAB!
SORRY... I'M KIDDING.

I KNOW. I'M JUST... NEVER MIND.
I'M HAVING A BAD DAY. EVERYTHING... FEELS OFF, Y'KNOW? LIKE SOMETHING MAJOR IS ABOUT TO HAPPEN.

IT'S JUST ANOTHER DAY, PEPPER. DON'T STRESS IT.
LOOK...YOU KNOW I LOVE YOU. DID YOU BRING THAT NEW SKIN? I SO WANT TO SEE THAT.
YEAH... HOLD ON.

SWEET! I CAN'T BELIEVE YOU EVEN GOT AHOLD OF THIS. THEY'RE SOLD OUT ON ALL THE SITES.

I'M NOT EVEN GONNA WAIT. LET'S TRY THIS SUCKER OUT RIGHT NOW...

OOOH...IT'S SLEEK...HOW DO I LOOK?

GOOFY. LIKE YOU WANT EVERYONE TO LOOK AT YOU.
YES. I TOTALLY DO WANT THAT.

WHY DIDN'T YOU GET ONE FOR YOURSELF? IT WOULD LOOK GREAT ON YOU.
ENH...

I STAND OUT MORE THAN I WANT ALREADY.
WILLOUGHBY HIGH SCHOOL
NEXT EXIT

I'M BACK. OH... ZOLA, THAT SKIN IS SWEET.
IT'S ON LOAN, BUT I LOVE IT.

I THINK STRONA WILL LEAVE YOU ALONE--AT LEAST FOR TODAY. SHE TRIED TO PICK ON THAT NEW ZARGIAN KID.
THE ONE WITH FOUR ARMS? PFF. THAT'S GOING TO GO BAD FOR STRONA.
PEPPER... YOU CAN'T LET YOURSELF BE PUSHED AROUND.

TALLY'S RIGHT. YOU HAVE TO STAND UP FOR YOURSELF.
I KNOW...
IT'S JUST...
...IT'S HARD TO ARGUE WITH HER. SHE'S NOT TOTALLY WRONG.
WELL... I MEAN...

...WHAT WOULD SUPERNOVA DO?

HM.

THAT **REALLY** DEPENDS ON WHICH **ERA. GOLDEN AGE** SUPERNOVA WOULD FLY HER BULLIES TO THE **REHABILITORIUM,** WHERE THEY WOULD LEARN TO BE BETTER PEOPLE.
SUPER-NOVA!

THAT'S JUST WEIRD. **WHY** DID I ASK?
I HAVE **NO IDEA.**
MODERN AGE SUPERNOVA WOULD PUNCH THEM, THOUGH.

SEE... **NOW** WE'RE--

SHE'D PUNCH THEM WITH **RAINBOWS.**
NOPE. **NEVER MIND.**

PEPPER...YOU **CAN'T** HIDE FROM EVERY PROBLEM.

AT SOME POINT, YOU *HAVE* TO LIVE IN THE *REAL* *WORLD.*

GOOD AND EVIL.
WILLOUGHBY
WILLOUGHBY
PLEASE REPORT TO CLASS
DARKNESS AND LIGHT.
THE REALM OF THE VOID GROWS STRONGER.
THE POWER OF THE SUNS WE MUST REIGNITE.

STUDENTS...OPEN YOUR SCREENS TO TAB 478.B.
PLEASE NOTE--YOUR GRADES FOR THIS SESSION WILL BE CALCULATED ON A *CURVE.* YOUR RETENTION SKILLS, THOUGH *WOEFULLY* UNDERDEVELOPED, ARE SUFFICIENT FOR THESE *SIMPLE* SUBJECTS.
NOW...
·MOON HISTORY·

...WHO CAN TELL ME WHAT YEAR THE EXODUS FROM *OLD EARTH* OCCURRED?

OH! UH...*PROFESSOR KILLIAN,* I KNOW...IT WAS, LIKE, 2792!

HM. AN *ADEQUATE* ANSWER FOR A LOW-LEVEL QUESTION.
AND CAN ANYONE NAME THE *ORIGINAL* THREE COLONY WORLDS?

ANYONE?

UH...DRAXUS, CENTAURI, AND THE...UM...OLD MOON?
PFF. "OLD MOON?" IF YOU MEAN ANDRONI MAJOR, THEN... YES. HALF CREDIT.

THE FIRST FAMOUS RESIDENT OF ANDRONI MAJOR WAS...?
PEPPER PAGE...?

AH... ME?
MUST I REPEAT THE QUESTION?
I WAS JUST...Y'KNOW? UM...MAYBE...

HEY!

PERHAPS YOU WOULD CARE TO CEASE READING THIS CARTOON MAGAZINE AND ANSWER THE QUESTION?
SUPER-NOVA!
I WILL! I REALLY WILL!
ANDRONI MAJOR... UM...
THIS IS QUITE DISAPPOINTING, PEPPER. WE'VE ALREADY--

WAIT...ANDRONI MAJOR...ISSUE 373! SUPERNOVA TEAMED UP WITH THE ALPHA SQUAD AND CELEBRATED THE RIBBON-CUTTING CEREMONY...

THIS IS HISTORY, MISS PAGE...NOT A DISCUSSION ON DEVIANT AND OUT-DATED POP CULTURE MAGAZINES.
BUT I KNOW THIS...I JUST...

THEY HAD A SPECIAL REAL-WORLD GUEST THAT ISSUE! AND...IT RELATES. IT TOTALLY RELATES...

IT WAS A CHARITY COVER... OMIGOSH...IT WAS DRAWN BY AL PLASTINO AND...UM... PETER DAVID DID THE SCRIPT...
NOT THE ORIGINAL PLASTINO OR DAVID, I MEAN. THEY WERE LONG DEAD. BUT... THEIR CLONES...

ENOUGH! ANSWER THE QUESTION OR I WILL HAVE YOU REMOVED FROM THIS CLASS!
WHO WAS THE FIRST FAMOUS RESIDENT TO COLONIZE ANDRONI MAJOR?!

IT WAS A CHARITY COVER AND THE GUEST STAR WAS...
THADDEUS MARTINEZ! THE INVENTOR OF ARTIFICIAL GRAVITY--HE WAS THE FIRST COLONIST!

SO... UH...
THAT'S... RIGHT. RIGHT?

PLAF!

HM.
MARTINEZ WAS THE FIRST COLONIST. AND HE WAS FAMOUS.
BUT...THE ASTROPILOT TRACI HUI ARRIVED BEFOREHAND TO SET UP THE COLONY, WHERE SHE SPENT HER REMAINING DAYS.
TRAGICALLY, IT SEEMS HER VALUABLE CONTRIBUTIONS TO THE MISSION WERE OVERLOOKED BY MISTERS PLASTINO AND DAVID. A PITY.

YOU CAN'T BELIEVE EVERYTHING YOU READ, MISS PAGE. HALF CREDIT ONLY!
HA HA HA HA HA HA HA

HA HA HA HA HA

8:00--
TRANSDIMENSIONAL SCIENCE:
AS YOU CAN SEE FROM THE CHART, THE ANCIENT TERRAN BOVINES WERE **WOEFULLY** UNDER-DEVELOPED, WITH ONLY FOUR STOMACHS...

8:45--
INTERGALACTIC ECONOMICS:
OF COURSE, SOCIETY HAS **EVOLVED** PAST SUCH SIMPLE FORMS OF CURRENCY, AND INSTEAD DEPENDS ON A SOPHISTICATED METRIC OF **INTANGIBLE** DEBT...

9:30--
INTERSTELLAR LANGUAGES:
AS WE ALL KNOW, ARTIFICIAL COMPONENTS HAVE OBVIOUSLY RENDERED MULTIPLE LANGUAGES **MOOT.** HOWEVER...

10:15--
SPACE MUSIC:
AND THOUGH THE METAL HORN OF THE TRIAMBULOTHON IS CONSIDERED ONE OF THE MOST **HARMONIC** WIND INSTRUMENTS KNOWN TO EXIST, THE STRANGE CREATURE IS **LARGELY** EXTINCT...

11:00--
ADVANCED
ROBOTICS...
11:30--
TERRESTRIAL
GEOPHYSICS...

12:00--
INTERTRANSDIMENSIONAL
GEOGRAPHY...

12:30--
SPACE
POTTERY...

1:15--
QUASI-POLITICAL
SCIENCE...

2:15--
ANTIMATTER
CALLIGRAPHY...

SUPERNOVA, YOU HAVE TO TRUST ME!
THE CURSE OF THE BRONZE BEETLE HAS BEEN LIFTED!
I'M MYSELF AGAIN -- I'M STEVE SIRIUS!
DO I DARE?
PFF...
HOW DOES SHE *ALWAYS* END UP WITH STEVE SIRIUS, ANYWAY?

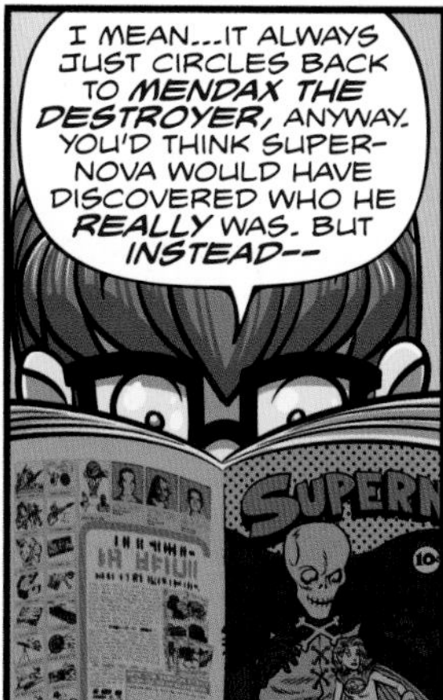

THAT'S PROFESSOR KILLIAN. I HAVE EARNED MY TITLE, PLEASE DO NOT IGNORE IT.
UH... YEAH. YES, SIR. PROFESSOR. SIR.
I SEE YOU REMAIN HOPELESSLY ENGAGED IN THE REALM OF MAKE-BELIEVE.
IT'S... COMICS. YOU KNOW...

MAY I?
UM...

SUPERNOVA.
THE FIRST APPEARANCE OF THE GIGGLING SKULL.
A RARE ORIGINAL COPY.
YOU KNOW... COMICS? YOU--

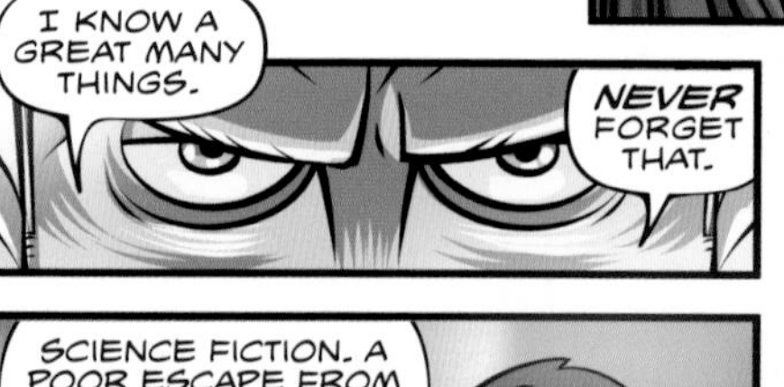
I KNOW A GREAT MANY THINGS.
NEVER FORGET THAT.

SCIENCE FICTION. A POOR ESCAPE FROM THE INTELLECTUAL REALM OF TRUE SCIENCE.
JUVENILE AND IMMATURE HOBBY, FOR THE WEAK OF WILL AND MIND.

TO THAT END...I WAS SEEKING YOU.
ME?

I WILL BE CONDUCTING AN IMPORTANT EXPERIMENT ON THE PRACTICAL MECHANICS OF QUANTUM ENTANGLEMENT UTILIZING THE KIRBY EQUATION.

THE EXACT SOLUTION TO THE THEOREM HAS NEVER BEEN CONFIRMED. BUT I AM CLOSE...
AND YOU, MISS PAGE, WILL HELP ME--
I WILL? I MEAN... ME? YOU THINK I COULD ASSIST YOU IN YOUR RESEARCH?

OHMIGOSH I ALWAYS WANTED TO BE A RESEARCHER. SUPERNOVA WAS A SCIENCE RESEARCHER, TOO, AND SHE'S, LIKE, MY HERO. I COULD BE LIKE HER--

AMUSING AS IT IS TO LISTEN TO YOUR DELUSIONS OF GRANDEUR, YOU MISUNDER-STAND.
I WILL REQUIRE LABORATORY 3, LOCATED IN THE SCIENCE BUILDING, TO BE SCRUBBED DOWN TOMORROW BEFORE CLASS.

...OH.

I--YOU NEED...A JANITOR?

AT LAST YOU GRASP THE OBVIOUS. YES. USE THIS KEY CODE TO ACCESS MY WORK-ROOM AT 0700 HOURS.
BE PRECISE. MY EXPERIMENTS ARE NOT TO BE...INTERRUPTED.

REMEMBER...YOUR PERFORMANCE COUNTS AGAINST YOUR FINAL GRADE. AND AFTER YOUR PERFORMANCE TODAY...
TOSS!
LET'S JUST SAY... YOU CANNOT AFFORD ANOTHER MISSTEP.
EEP!

AW... POOR COMIC.
YOU GET A CREASE?

NOT BAD...I CAN PRESS IT BETWEEN A COUPLE BOARDS FOR A FEW DAYS. SHOULD BE MOSTLY SMOOTHED OUT AFTER--

'SUP, FANGIRL!
BAP!
AHH!

GUH!!

GASP!
MY COMICS!

OKAY...I CAN SAVE THEM...SOON AS THE HALL CLEARS...
THEY'RE STILL MINT...
...MAYBE NEAR MINT...

...VERY GOOD...
...POOR. VERY POOR.

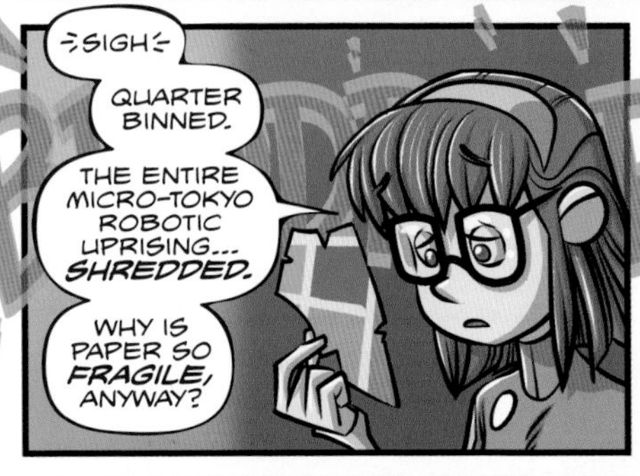
SIGH
QUARTER BINNED.
THE ENTIRE MICRO-TOKYO ROBOTIC UPRISING... SHREDDED.
WHY IS PAPER SO FRAGILE, ANYWAY?

RiNG
WAIT? THE BELL?! THE BELL!!

THE HOLO-GAME!!!

LATER...
ARGENT
CINEMA CLASSICS WEEK
SUPERNOVA!
ARGENT
SUPERNOVA!

ATER 2
PEPPER?

YOU MISSED THE *HOLO-GAME...* AND THE BUS. WE FIGURED WE SHOULD WAIT FOR YOU...AND YOU *STILL* DIDN'T SHOW.
...THE SCHOOL TRACKER PINGED YOU *HERE...*
WHICH WAS *INCREDIBLY* UNSURPRISING.

YEAH.

I'M HERE.

PEPPER...
SOO... WATCHING VIDS ALONE. DOING GREAT?
...YEAH.

IT'S THE 25TH-CENTURY REBOOT OF THE CLASSIC *SUPERNOVA: THE MOTION PICTURE.* THE *GOOD* ONE. NOT THAT *REALLY BAD* ONE WITH ALL THE LASERS.

MENDAX, YOU FIEND! YOU'LL NEVER DESTROY THE EARTH!
SEE...IT'S A TOTALLY FAITHFUL ADAPTATION. NOT LIKE THE ***RECENT*** VERSIONS--THOSE ***COMPLETELY*** CHANGED THE STORY.
WHY ARE YOU IN HERE? THE BUS--
WE CAN GET A CAR. MY PARENTS WILL DRIVE YOU--

TO THE ***ORPHANAGE.***
WELL...

I DON'T ***BELONG*** THERE. I DON'T BELONG ***HERE.***

I DON'T BELONG ***ANYWHERE.***

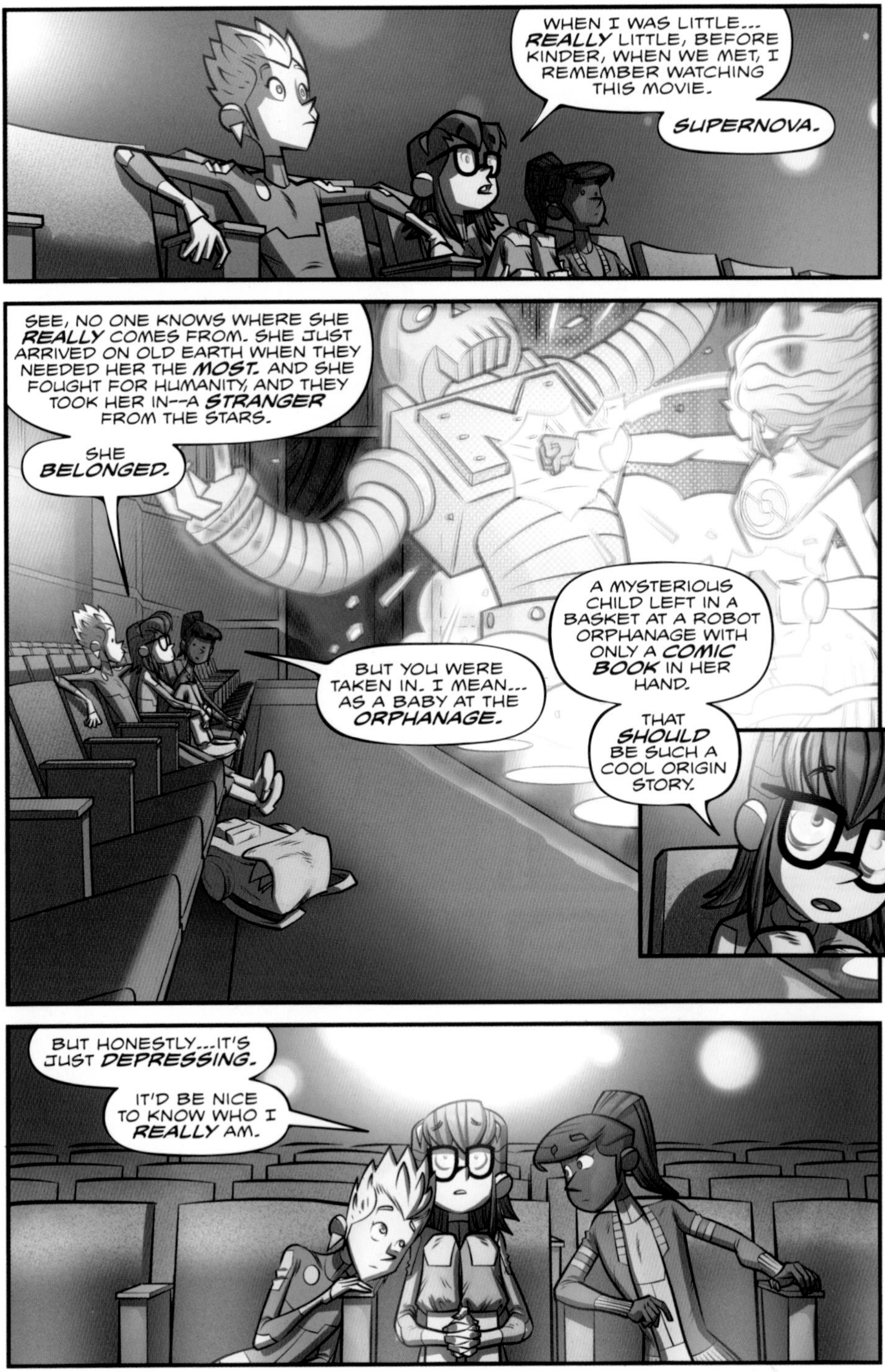

SEE, NO ONE KNOWS WHERE SHE REALLY COMES FROM. SHE JUST ARRIVED ON OLD EARTH WHEN THEY NEEDED HER THE MOST. AND SHE FOUGHT FOR HUMANITY, AND THEY TOOK HER IN--A STRANGER FROM THE STARS.

SHE BELONGED.

BUT YOU WERE TAKEN IN. I MEAN... AS A BABY AT THE ORPHANAGE.

A MYSTERIOUS CHILD LEFT IN A BASKET AT A ROBOT ORPHANAGE WITH ONLY A COMIC BOOK IN HER HAND.

THAT SHOULD BE SUCH A COOL ORIGIN STORY.

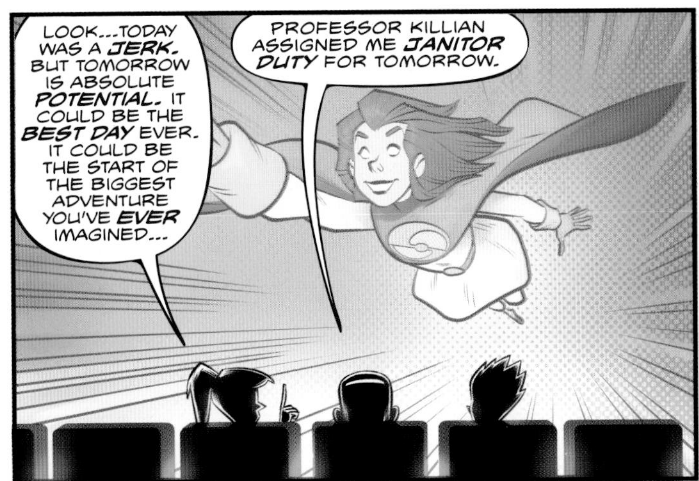
LOOK...TODAY WAS A JERK. BUT TOMORROW IS ABSOLUTE POTENTIAL. IT COULD BE THE BEST DAY EVER. IT COULD BE THE START OF THE BIGGEST ADVENTURE YOU'VE EVER IMAGINED...
PROFESSOR KILLIAN ASSIGNED ME JANITOR DUTY FOR TOMORROW.

WELL...THAT MIGHT BE LESS OF AN ADVENTURE. STILL...

IT'S NOT JUST THAT. I FEEL LIKE SOMETHING... SOMETHING BAD IS GOING TO HAPPEN. I KNOW I FEEL LIKE THAT A LOT...BUT ESPECIALLY TODAY.
WHEN I READ THE COMICS OR WATCH THE MOVIES...I FEEL LIKE EVERYTHING IS RIGHT.

KILLIAN THINKS I'M AN IDIOT FOR EVEN READING THEM.
WHATEVER! LIKE BEING A TEACHER MAKES HIM SO SMART? PFF!
PEOPLE TREAT BEING SHY LIKES IT'S SOME KIND OF CRIME...
I KNOW...

BUT RUNNING AWAY AND HIDING FROM YOUR PROBLEMS...THEY'RE NOT GOING TO GO AWAY UNLESS YOU DO SOMETHING ABOUT THEM.
YEAH...

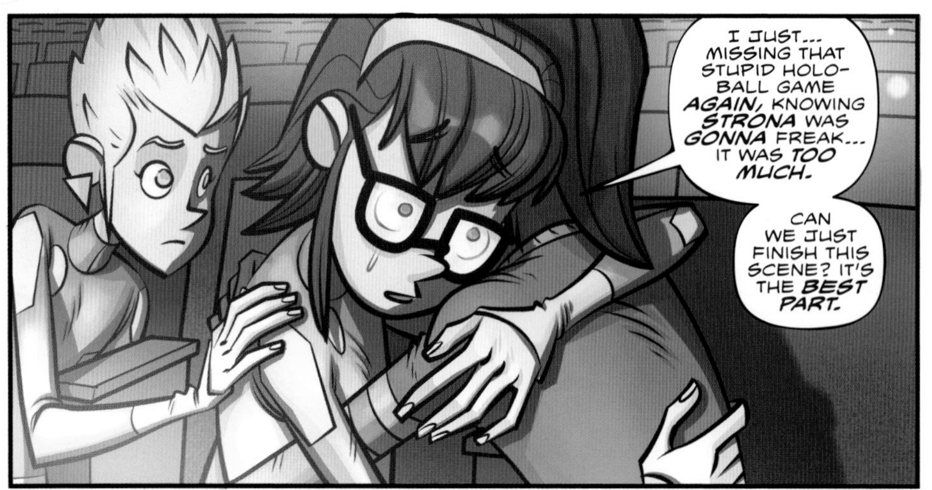

I WON'T GIVE UP, MENDAX. NOT TODAY...NOT TOMORROW. BECAUSE I DON'T FIGHT FOR MYSELF...

I FIGHT FOR WHAT IS RIGHT!

I FIGHT FOR WHAT IS **RIGHT.**

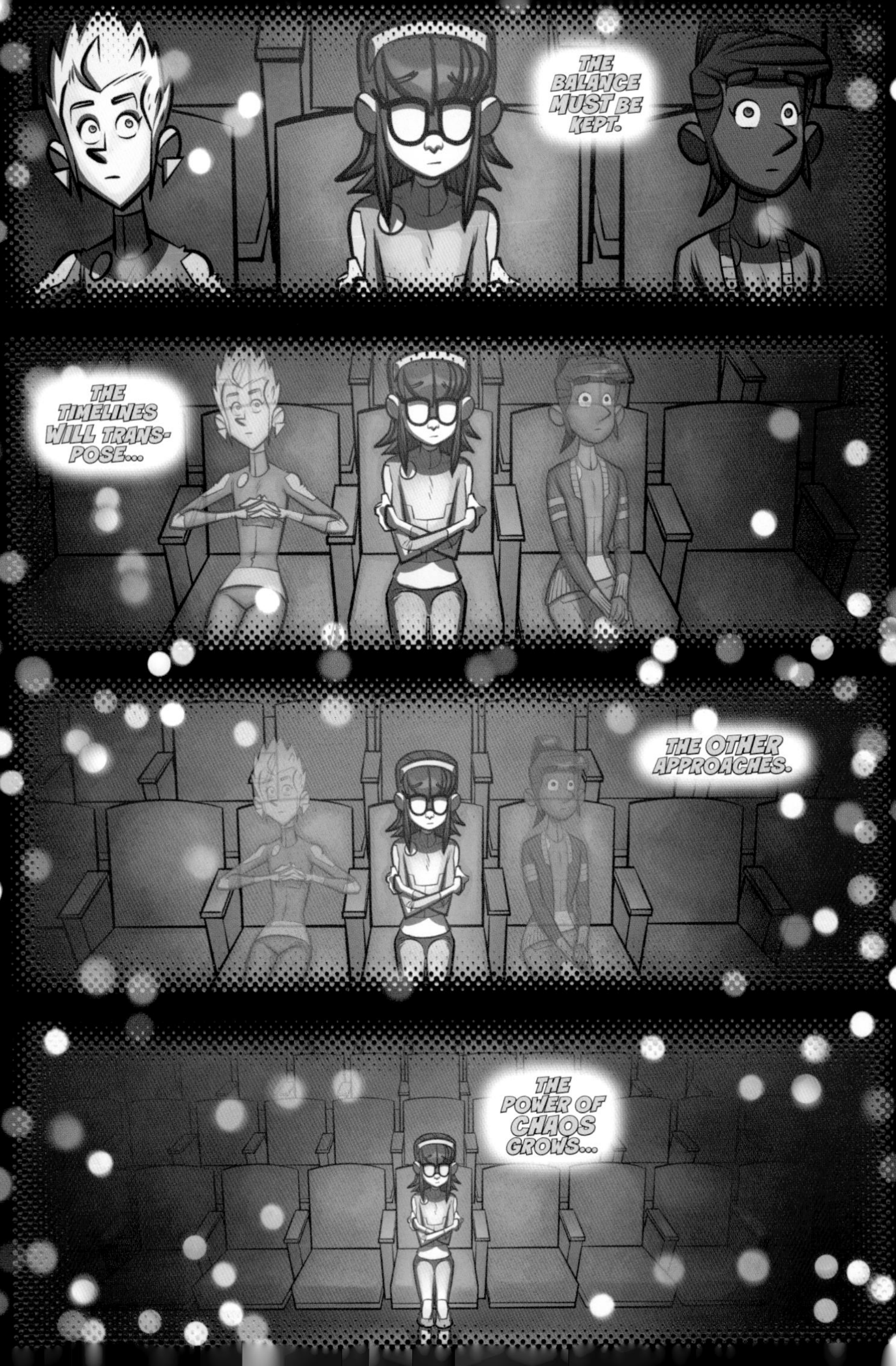

THE BALANCE MUST BE KEPT.

THE TIMELINES WILL TRANS-POSE...

THE OTHER APPROACHES.

"ECLIPSA, NO! WE DON'T HAVE TO FIGHT! WE CAN ***HELP*** EACH OTHER!"

"SUPERNOVA... YOU'RE SO BLIND! WE EXIST IN ***OPPOSITION!*** WE CAN ***NEVER*** BE FRIENDS!"

SPORT DOME

BLURG! WHY??
WHA...?
PICKLES... LETTUCE...
...OH NO.

I'M COVERED IN SANDWICH?!
THIS... THIS IS--

JUSTICE?
JUST RETURNING YOUR LUNCH, ZOLA. PLUS, I'VE GOT SOME UNFINISHED BUSINESS WITH THE COMIC GEEK YOU'RE PROTECTING.
STRONA, ENOUGH. THIS IS ALL GOING TOO FAR...

TOO FAR, TALLY? THAT STUPID ORPHAN SKIPPED THE GAME TODAY. SHE COST US THE REGIONALS!

NO ONE CARES ABOUT YOUR HOLO-BALL GAME! IT'S BARELY EVEN A REAL SPORT!

ARE YOU SERIOUS? HOLO-BALL IS THE FIFTH MOST POPULAR SPORT IN THE AFFILIATED UNION OF PLANETS!
FOURTH IF YOU COUNT THE ROBOT LEAGUES!

THERE'S ONLY SEVEN PLANETS IN THE UNION! THAT LEAVES LIKE... MORE THAN 200 OTHER INHABITED SYSTEMS!
MATH ISN'T IMPORTANT HERE! PEPPER FLAKED ON OUR GAME, AND THAT'S NOT COOL!

YOU'RE RIGHT...
I FORGOT... AND...I'M SORRY...

"SORRY" DOESN'T GET US BACK IN THE GAME--YOU GOTTA PAY FOR WHAT YOU DID!
THIS IS IT, PEPPER... STAND UP FOR YOUR-SELF!
WHAT?
ZOLA'S RIGHT! YOU CAN'T LET STRONA BULLY YOU!
WHAT? NO! ZOLA'S WRONG! I CAN TOTALLY LET STRONA BULLY ME!

YOU CAN'T LIVE YOUR WHOLE LIFE BEING AFRAID! I MEAN...WHAT WOULD SUPER-NOVA DO?
REVERSE THE TIME STREAM? EXPOSE HERSELF TO NEUTRONIOXIUM SO SHE CAN GAIN NEW SUPERPOWERS?
I DUNNO... THERE'S A LOT OF OPTIONS THERE! NONE OF WHICH INVOLVE ME HAVING TO GET PUNCHED BY STRONA!

PFF. THAT'S WHAT I *THOUGHT*.

SNAP!

UM... GUYS...?

AW, MAN...THAT KID WITH THE FOUR ARMS *JOINED* HER SPORTS GANG! NO FAIR!
I THINK MAYBE WE SHOULD *GO*.

THEY'RE MONSTERS! MONSTERS!

YEAH, TALLY, WELCOME TO HIGH SCHOOL. THANKS FOR FINALLY JOINING US!

JUST RUN!

HOW ARE THEY STILL THROWING BALLS AT US?!
THEY'RE MADE OF HARD LIGHT! THEY'LL NEVER RUN OUT!
FOLLOW ME! HURRY!
WHERE ARE WE GOING?
ANYWHERE ELSE!
THIS IS ALL MY FAULT...I'M SORRY...I'M SORRY...

WHERE'D THEY GO?
I THINK WE HIT 'EM HARD ENOUGH...
NO...

WE COULD HAVE MADE DIVISION THIS YEAR...THEN NEXT YEAR WE COULD HAVE MADE FIRST TIER.
SO...?
SO WE FIND THE STUPID ORPHAN AND WE MAKE HER SEE THE POWER OF TEAMWORK. RIGHT IN HER STUPID FACE.

SHE CAN'T RUN FOREVER...

UGH. COULD YOU MAYBE PICK SOME LESS ATHLETIC ENEMIES NEXT TIME?
WHY DID YOU RUN, PEPPER? THAT JUST MAKES IT ALL WORSE!
I DIDN'T WANT TO GET HIT IN THE FACE WITH SPORTS EQUIPMENT!

THAT'S A SOLID POINT.
WE JUST NEED TO HIDE UNTIL THEY GIVE UP LOOKING.
THIS...THIS IS THE SCIENCE BUILDING...

YEAH... SUPER OBSERVANT, PEPPER. THIS IS TOTALLY THE SCIENCE BUILDING.
DOES IT MATTER? IT'S AFTER HOURS, EVERYTHING'S LOCKED UP.
BUT I HAVE A KEY CARD, SO I CAN DO THE JANITOR STUFF TOMORROW! IT'S NOT VALID UNTIL 0700 THOUGH...

HM.
I THINK I HAVE A PLAN...

IT IS TIME.
IT HAS ALWAYS BEEN TIME.
SHE REMAINS A PRISONER OF HER FEAR.
SHE WILL OVERCOME THIS. SHE IS READY.
THE MOMENT IS NEARLY HERE.

THIS IS A TERRIBLE PLAN.
ALMOST GOT IT.
HURRY BEFORE THEY COME BACK...
OH...I'M JUST HACKING THE SCHOOL LOCKS SLOW-LIKE FOR FUN. BECAUSE WHY NOT?

THIS IS AGAINST THE LAW. IF WE GET CAUGHT, WE'LL BE SUSPENDED OR SOMETHING...
OR SOMETHING? SOMETHING WORSE THAN SUSPENSION? THEY CAN DO THAT? LIKE PRISON? ARE WE GOING TO PRISON?!
TOO FAR, PEPPER.

OHMIGOSH...I'M GOING TO BE IN PRISON FOREVER AND I'M GOING TO HAVE TO LEARN TO MAKE LICENSE PLATES AND WEAR BLACK AND WHITE STRIPES--
PEPPER!

HA! HERE WE GO...

FSSSSHHHHHHHH!
GOT IT!

HOW ARE WE SUPPOSED TO GET PAST THE SECURITY-BOTS?
I'M SERIOUS. SOMETHING ABOUT THIS FEELS REALLY, REALLY BAD.
THAT'S THE EASY PART-- PEPPER'S HALL PASS.

BUT IT'S CODED FOR HER...
YEAH, BUT HALL PASSES ARE LOW ENCRYPTION. THE HARD PART IS GETTING ONE.

LOOK OUT!

ALERT! ALERT!
UGH. CHILL, PEPPER. IT'S NOT THAT BIG A DEAL.

I'M TELLING YOU, WE SHOULDN'T BE HERE! DON'T EITHER OF YOU FEEL HOW WRONG THIS IS?
JUST RELAX!
WHEN HAVE I EVER?

UNAUTHORIZED MINORS DETECTED. YOU HAVE TEN SECONDS TO COMPLY WITH PROTOCOL 7. ESTABLISH AUTHORIZATION.

CODE DELTA-KARZ OMEGA E11957. AUTHORIZATION EQUALS **BLUE.**

WE GOOD, ROBOT?
EEP.
UM...
CALCULATING...

AUTHORIZATION **ACCEPTED.** ENJOY YOUR AFTER-HOURS SCHOOL VISIT, STUDENTS.

SEE?

YOU HAD **NO IDEA** THAT WAS GOING TO WORK.
NO. NO I DID **NOT.**
SHOULDN'T BE HERE...

SOMETHING...

DO YOU **HEAR** SOMETHING?

AM I THE ONLY ONE WHO **FEELS** THIS...

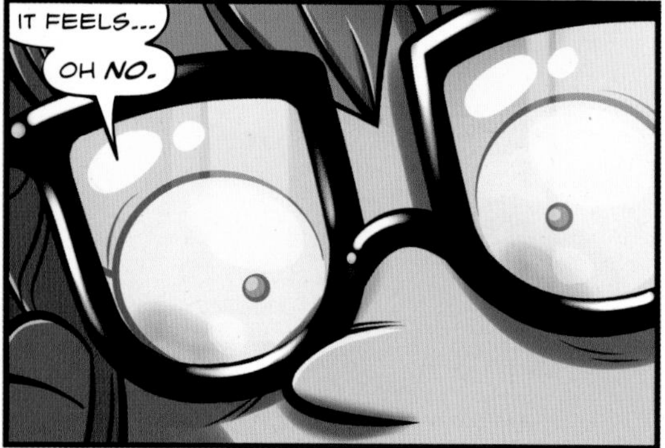
IT FEELS...
OH **NO.**

TALLY! ZOLA! HIDE! QUICK!
WHAT NOW?
WE HAVE A HALL PASS! WHAT IS YOUR PROBLEM?
IT'S NOT A SECURI-TY-BOT...
...IT'S MISTER KILLIAN!
YOU MEAN PROFESSOR...
NOT THE POINT, TALLY.
WHAT'S HE DOING?
WORK? GRADING PAPERS? WHO KNOWS?
HE HAS A CAT. IN A CAGE.

COME ON...
BUT THE CAT!

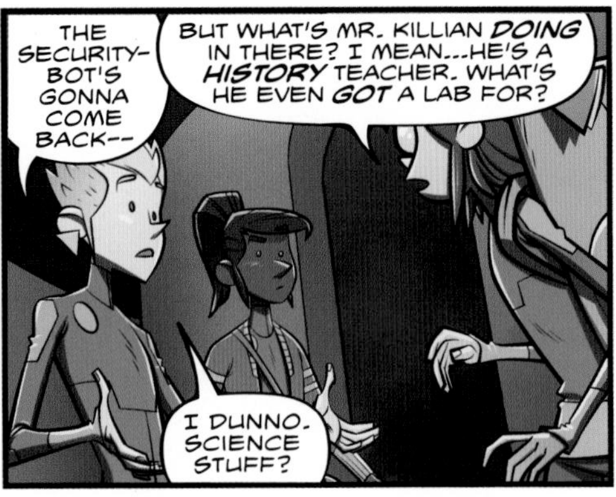
THE SECURITY-BOT'S GONNA COME BACK--
BUT WHAT'S MR. KILLIAN DOING IN THERE? I MEAN...HE'S A HISTORY TEACHER. WHAT'S HE EVEN GOT A LAB FOR?
I DUNNO. SCIENCE STUFF?

COME ON!
PEPPER...

...WAIT!
I'VE BEEN FEELING WEIRD, LIKE...ALL DAY. AND THIS IS...
I JUST WANT TO SEE THIS.

V = 2 π 2 R 3...
THAT SHOULD DO IT!
ZZZZRAAAZZZAPP!
HOLY MONKEYS...

THIS LAB...
IT'S LIKE SOMETHING OUT OF A COMIC BOOK!

BUT WHAT'S HE DOING?
I HAVE **NO IDEA.**

HM. **ALMOST** PERFECT.
JUST **NEED** TO REVERSE THE POLARITY OF THE **NEUTRON FLOW...**

INTERESTING...

ZZZZZZZZZZZZZZZZZZZ

VORP!

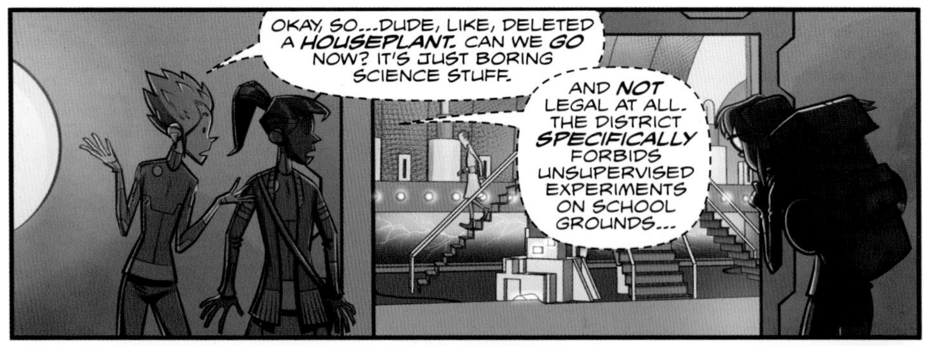
OKAY, SO... DUDE, LIKE, DELETED A HOUSEPLANT. CAN WE GO NOW? IT'S JUST BORING SCIENCE STUFF.
AND NOT LEGAL AT ALL. THE DISTRICT SPECIFICALLY FORBIDS UNSUPERVISED EXPERIMENTS ON SCHOOL GROUNDS...

YES.
PERHAPS A SLIGHT VARIATION TO THE MODULATION OF THE ENERGY FIELD...

...AND WE'LL BE READY FOR A TRUE TEST OF THE QUANTUM FIELD MANIPULATOR.
MEW?

UHH...
NO!
WHOA. HE'S LIKE A LEGIT MAD SCIENTIST? NO WAY THIS IS REAL...

THE FOOLS DOUBTED MY RESEARCH. WELL...
ONCE AND FOR ALL, THIS WILL PROVE THAT IT'S ALL TRUE. IT'S ALL REAL...

THE TEST SUBJECT IS HEALTHY...AND WELL PREPARED FOR THE PROCESS.
THAT WILL LEAVE ONLY ONE MORE HURDLE. ONE THAT WILL BE PASSED COME THE MORNING.
A HUMAN SUBJECT.

PEPPER!
WHAT ARE YOU DOING?!
SHH... JUST GIVE ME A SECOND!

YOU CAN'T!
DON'T!
IT'LL BE OKAY!
I HAVE BEEN QUITE LUCKY, FOR I BEGAN TO DOUBT I WOULD EVER FIND A SUITABLE... CANDIDATE.

LUCKILY...THIS ONE IS UNLIKELY TO BE MISSED. HER NAME IS--
KLIK!

EH?

UM...
MEW!
PEPPER PAGE?!!

MISTER KILLIAN! I MEAN, PROFESSOR! I MEAN--
--YOU CAN'T DISINTEGRATE THIS CAT!
MEW?

CHILD, REMOVE YOURSELF FROM THE QUANTUM CHAMBER AT ONCE! IT IS A DELICATE PIECE OF MACHINERY THAT IS SET TO--

SYSTEM CHECK COMPLETE. INITIATING SEQUENCE S-131...
WHA?
TIK

WHAT JUST--? EVERYTHING JUST WENT TINGLY. TINGLY AND SPARKLY...
YOU... FOOL!

I HAVE WORKED FOR YEARS... YEARS! ALL TO SEE A LIFETIME OF SCIENCE... WASTED! BECAUSE OF A STUPID CHILD!

I'M SORRY, PROFESSOR... I CAN'T LET YOU HURT THIS CAT. I...I'M SUPPOSED TO STAND UP FOR...FOR THINGS.

IT'S... WHAT'S RIGHT.

HOW UTTERLY NOBLE. HOW COMPLETELY POINTLESS.
YOU HAVE CONDEMNED YOURSELF TO DOOM, CHILD.

THE CAT--
PFF. THE CAT IS NOT WHAT YOU SHOULD BE CONCERNED ABOUT. YOU HAVE ENTERED A GRAVITATIONAL NEXUS POINT. AND IT IS PREPARING TO ACTIVATE.

YOU MEAN LIKE... A BLACK HOLE? I'M TRAPPED IN A BLACK HOLE?!
HM. YOUR GRASP IS PRIMITIVE, BUT...BEYOND AVERAGE. YES. YOU HAVE BEEN SEPARATED FROM THIS PLANE OF EXISTENCE. YOU ARE TUMBLING AWAY WITHIN ANOTHER DIMENSION, EVEN AS WE SPEAK.
I WILL RECORD YOUR FINAL MOMENTS...IN THE INTEREST OF SCIENCE. BUT I'M AFRAID THIS IS THE END FOR YOU, PEPPER PAGE.

WHAT?
NO!
AH...THERE ARE MORE OF YOU. OF COURSE.

AND DO ANY OF YOU COMPREHEND THE WORK YOU HAVE DISRUPTED? UNACCEPTABLE...

I CAN'T GET ANY CLOSER! IT'S LIKE I'M BEING PUSHED BACKWARD!
WHAT IS **WRONG** WITH YOU?! LET HER OUT! **NOW!!**

IF I COULD, I **WOULD.** YOUR FRIEND HAS **DESTROYED** A LIFETIME OF WORK!
FOR DECADES I WORKED, DEVOTING MYSELF TO UNLOCKING THE **MYSTERIES OF TIME...** OPENING THE DOORWAY INTO THE REALM **BEYOND** THE PHYSICAL. I BORROWED AND BEGGED AND **STOLE** TO POSITION MYSELF IN **THIS** MOMENT. A MOMENT NOW **STOLEN** FROM ME!

IT'S STARTING...
THIS IS ALL MY FAULT... MY FAULT!

I'M **SORRY...**

THERE MUST BE SOME-THING... SOME WAY TO SHUT IT DOWN!
THERE IS **NOT.**

...IS THAT ME? BUT I LOOK OLD! I'M SOMEWHERE...IN A HOUSE? WHOSE HOUSE IS THIS?

AH, INTERESTING. YOU ARE SEEING QUANTUM REALITIES. YOUR OWN FUTURE, NOW FOREVER DENIED YOU. YOU ARE SEEING THE LIFE YOU WOULD HAVE HAD.

I LOOK... HAPPY. I WAS GOING TO BE HAPPY.

THAT MUST BE VERY INTERESTING FOR YOU. FOR ME IT IS SIMPLY A ***DISTRACTION.*** UNDERSTAND THIS: YOUR MEDDLING MAY HAVE COST ME TIME, BUT I WILL STILL PREVAIL.

YOU'RE A ***MONSTER!***
PERHAPS.

GOODBYE, MISS PAGE...

I WILL ***NOT*** FORGET THIS.

...
...I DON'T WANT TO GO.

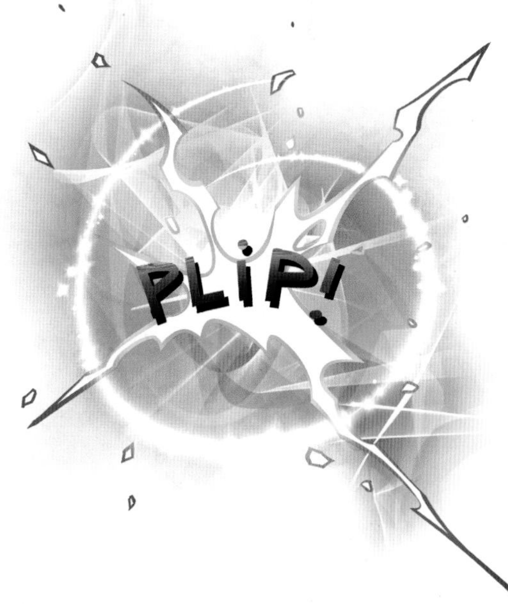
PLIP!

A HERO RISES!

NOT A DREAM! NOT AN IMAGINARY STORY!
YOU'RE ABOUT TO WITNESS THE BIRTH OF THE GREATEST HERO OF ALL TIME! READ ON FOR...
SUPERNOVA'S STARTLING SECRET ORIGIN!

A HERO RISES!
SUPERNOVA'S STARTLING SECRET ORIGIN!

A HERO RISES!
AAAAAAAAAAAAAHHHHHH!

I'M ALIVE?
I'M ALIVE!

I'M ALIVE, BUT I'M HURTLING THROUGH SPACE??

I HATE TODAY! I HATE IT! I HATE IT SO MUCH!

OH NO! CAT! STOP!
I'LL SAVE YOU!
MEW!

ALMOST... GOT...
...CAT!
ROWR?

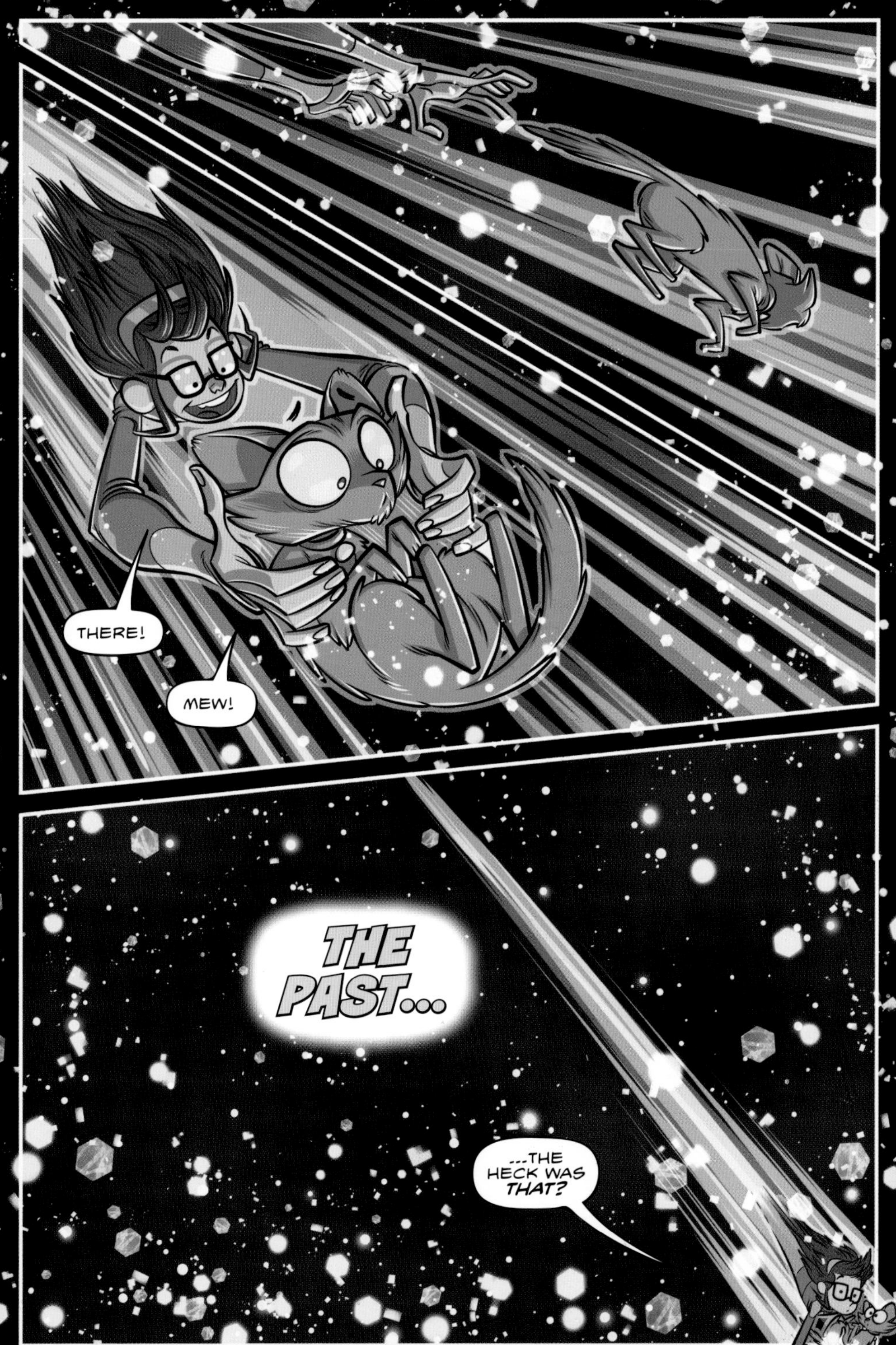
THERE!
MEW!
THE PAST...
...THE HECK WAS THAT?

AHH...
AAAHHH!
NOT FUN!
THE PRESENT...
UNF!

THE FUTURE...

ENTWINED.

THE GATEWAY IS OPEN.

THE STARS HAVE ALIGNED.

KBOOF!
PAF!
PAF!
PLAFF!
FUP!
FUP!
FWUMP!

THINGS...
...THINGS CAN STOP HAPPENING NOW.

BUT I'M ALIVE. I THINK I'M ALIVE.

OHMIGOSH.

WHERE THE HECK AM I?

OKAY...

SO...THIS IS WHAT, CAT? WE'RE ON ANOTHER PLANET? IN ANOTHER DIMENSION?
I'VE READ ENOUGH COMICS TO KNOW A TRIP THROUGH TIME AND SPACE WHEN I SEE ONE.

USUALLY THE HERO IN THE STORY GETS TELEPORTED TO SOME DISTANT REALM, HAS TO UNDERTAKE SOME SORT OF EPIC JOURNEY, DISCOVER THE SECRETS OF THE UNIVERSE, AND OPEN THE PORTAL BACK HOME.
THERE WAS A VOICE, SO WE'RE... SOMEWHERE...AND WE'RE NOT ALONE. WE JUST...JUST HAVE TO FIND WHO THE VOICE BELONGS TO.

THAT'S GOTTA BE WHAT THIS IS.
YUP.

THE QUESTS IN THE COMICS...

THEY ***USUALLY*** HAPPEN BETWEEN THE PANELS. BUT ***THIS...*** THIS IS TAKING FOREVER.

MAYBE...
MAYBE THIS ISN'T LIKE THE COMICS?
Z
KINDA MORE LIKE THE NOVELS...
HARD TO READ...
...AND THEY GO ON FOREVER.

I HOPE ZOLA AND TALLY ARE OKAY.
ZOLA ACTS SO STRONG, BUT SHE'S GOING TO FEEL SO ALONE. AND SHE'LL FEEL GUILTY. SHE ALWAYS DOES WHEN SHE GETS ME INTO TROUBLE.
I SHOULD HAVE TOLD HER--IT WASN'T HER FAULT.
I WISH I HAD.
TALLY WON'T BELIEVE IT.
SHE'LL LOOK FOR ME. SHE'S PROBABLY LOOKING RIGHT NOW.
I DON'T THINK SHE'S GOING TO FIND ME THIS TIME.

NO!

THAT'S--THAT'S *IMPOSSIBLE!*

...
WHOEVER IS OUT THERE... WHERE AM I? WHY IS THIS HAPPENING TO ME?
HELP ME.
I'M AFRAID... PLEASE...
UH...
RRRRRRRRRRUMMBLE

FEAR.
OHMIGOSH.
WHAT...WHAT IS THIS? WHO...YOU'RE NOT THE SAME VOICE. THE ONE FROM BEFORE--
YOUR FEAR...
IT CALLS TO US.
IT FEEDS...
YOUR FEAR...
YOUR POWER...
YOUR FATE...
BROKEN...
CHAOS.
NO...
NO NO NO...
YOU ARE HER.
...PLEASE.
THEY BROUGHT YOU HERE.
HOW FOOLISH...

WE SEE YOU.
WE FEEL YOU.
THEY THINK YOU WILL SAVE THEM.
BUT THEY ARE WEAK...
...AND YOU ARE RIGHT TO BE AFRAID.

YOU NEVER NEED... TO FEEL.
PLEASE... STOP...

...PLEASE.
ENOUGH!
HSSS!

THAT'S THE VOICE! THE FIRST ONE! FROM WHEN I WAS IN SPACE!

HEY! SPACE VOICE! ENOUGH WITH THE ZAPPING! JUST...JUST GET US OUT OF HERE!
MEW?
OHMIGOSH, I'M YELLING AT AN INVISIBLE VOICE FROM SPACE.
IS THAT RUDE? DO INVISIBLE SPACE VOICES HAVE FEELINGS?
SIGH
I WANNA GO HOME.
PLIP!

PLIP!

UNF!

GUH...
WAS THAT IT? I JUST HAD TO WISH MYSELF HOME AND I'M *BACK?* AND NOW I WAKE UP AND IT WAS ALL A *DREAM,* RIGHT?

OH.

OHMIGOSH!!
I *KNOW* THIS! I KNOW *WHERE I AM!*

THE...THIS IS THE SUPERSYMMETRY OF SUNS! THIS...
TALES TO LEAVE YOU STARSTRUCK, ISSUE 252!
THIS...
THIS IS FROM A COMIC BOOK!

SUPERNOVA.

UH...

...NO?

YES.

YOU ARE THE LAST HOPE.

THE SUPERNOVA WILL AWAKEN.

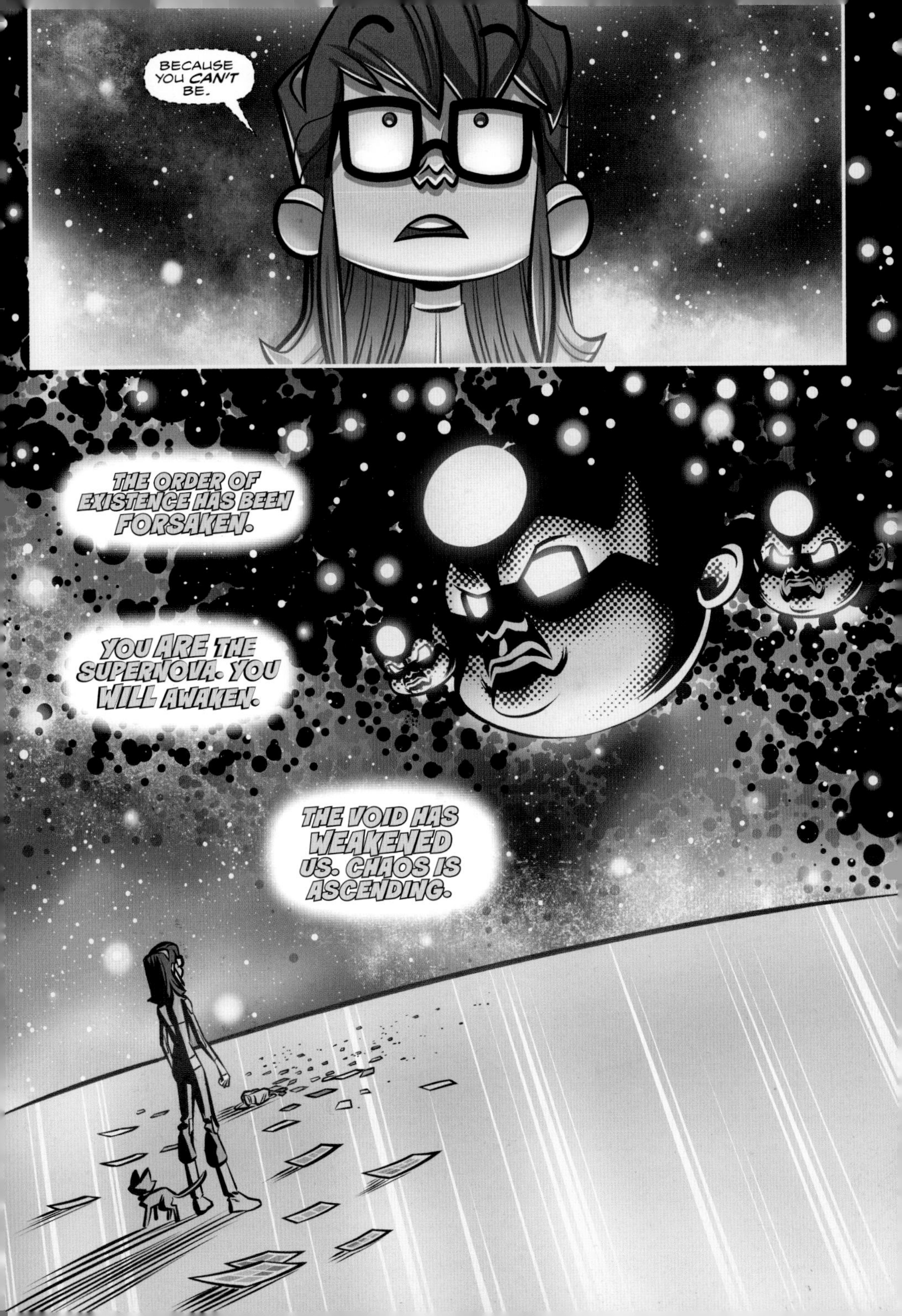

BECAUSE YOU CAN'T BE.
THE ORDER OF EXISTENCE HAS BEEN FORSAKEN.
YOU ARE THE SUPERNOVA. YOU WILL AWAKEN.
THE VOID HAS WEAKENED US. CHAOS IS ASCENDING.

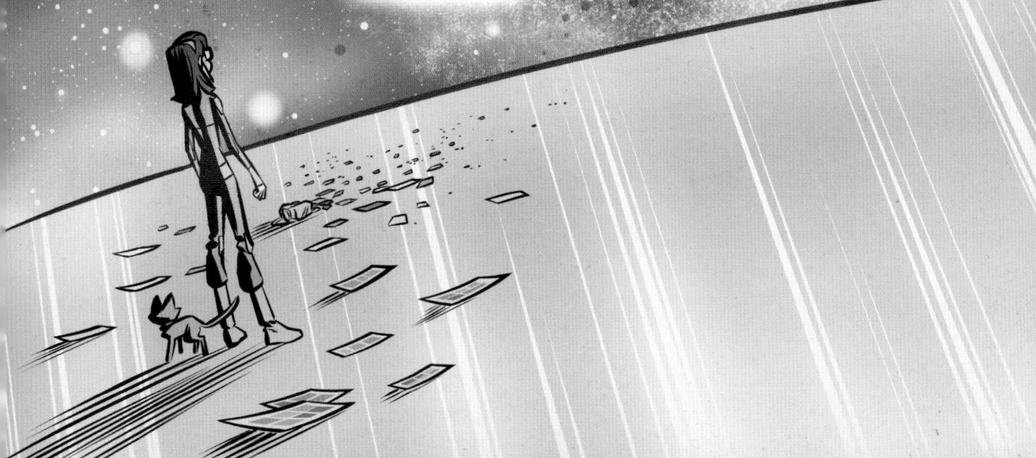

ORPHANAGE
FROM YOUR FIRST GASPING BREATH, TO YOUR LAST WEARY STEP...
WE HAVE HARKENED TO YOU, UNENDING.
BUT YOU HID FROM OTHERS AS YOU HID FROM YOURSELF. YOU ELUDED. WITHDREW.
AND SO WE REACHED ACROSS TIME AND SPACE...
...THROUGH THE ESCAPE YOU WOULD PURSUE.

THE ABUSE... THE TAUNTS... THE ISOLATION...
NEVER SHOOK THE NEED FOR JUSTICE YOU CRAVE.
BUT YOU MUST LET GO OF THAT WHICH HOLDS YOU BACK.
YOU MUST BE DARING. YOU MUST BE BRAVE.

MY MEMORIES... YOU MADE ME...I SAW IT ALL...MY WHOLE LIFE.
THE COSMIC RIFT WILL OPEN SOON. CHAOS WILL EMERGE.
YOU ARE THE ONLY HOPE AGAINST THIS ABOMINABLE SCOURGE.

AND NOW, AS OUR LIFE FORCE EBBS, YOU MUST HEED OUR ARDENT WORDS:
THE STARFORCE AND ITS SENTINEL MUST, AT LAST, CONVERGE.

THE CIRCLE OF YOUR EXISTENCE MUST ENDURE AND BE SUSTAINED.
ALIGNMENT MUST BE CALIBRATED.
ORDER MUST BE MAINTAINED.
YOU WILL FACE THE DESTROYER. YOU WILL FACE THE DECEIVER. NOW THE POWER YOU MUST CLAIM.
CALL YOUR STRENGTH, YOUR SKILL, YOUR WISDOM.
TAKE THE MANTLE.
SAY THE NAME.

THE DESTROYER? LIKE MENDAX? BUT WHAT'S THE DECEIVER?

SAY THE NAME.

WHAT?
I JUST WANT TO GO HOME! JUST...JUST SEND ME BACK!

WHATEVER YOU THINK I AM...
I'M NOT! OKAY? I'M JUST PEPPER PAGE!

THIS IS ALL **WRONG** ANYWAY! THE **OVERLORDS OF ORDER** WERE CREATED WHEN THE **OMPHALOS STONE** WAS SHATTERED.
AND THEN THEY **CREATED** THEIR AVATAR FROM **SPACE DUST!** SO I CAN'T...I **CAN'T** BE...
...SUPERNOVA?

THE NAME HAS BEEN SPOKEN.
THE PAST CANNOT BE CHANGED.
THE FUTURE HAS BEEN WRITTEN.
HARMONY SUSTAINED.

YOU WERE SUPERNOVA.
YOU WILL BE SUPERNOVA.
YOU HAVE ALWAYS BEEN SUPERNOVA.

THE CIRCLE HAS CLOSED.
DEFEAT THE CHAOS. RESTORE THE BALANCE.
THE TIME OF THE SUNS HAS PASSED...
...BUT EVIL MUST STILL BE OPPOSED.

BACK IN TIME
OH NO!
I'VE BEEN TRAPPED IN THE ANCIENT PAST!
I'VE GOT TO GET BACK HOME!

BACK IN TIME
I'VE BEEN TRAPPED IN THE ANCIENT PAST!
OH NO!
I'VE GOT GET BACK HOME!

BLURG...

WELL, THAT WAS A STUPID DREAM...
WHEN I GET HOME FROM THIS OLD-TIMEY CITY I'LL HAVE TO WRITE IT ALL--

OLD... TIMEY... CITY?

I'M IN AN OLD-TIMEY CITY! WITH BIG BOXY BUILDINGS AND NO FLYING CARS!
WHAT?!

THOSE STUPID GIANT BABY HEADS SENT ME TO THE PAST?! THEY'VE GOT BRAINS THE SIZE OF MY SCHOOL! HOW COULD THEY SEND ME TO THE WRONG PLACE?!
I MEAN, FIRST THEY THINK I'M A SUPERHERO, AND THEN--

WHAT.
WHAT.
WHAT.
OH NO!

WHAT THE HECK IS HAPPENING TO ME??!

OR IT'S LIKE IN THE *COMICS!* LIKE, A *DREAM SEQUENCE* OR...

OH NO! *MY COMICS!*

WAIT... HERE'S SOME OF THEM... ISSUE 3 OF THE *SUPER SCARY MONSTER SHOW?*
PFF...I MEAN, IT'S *OKAY,* BUT THE BACKUP APPEARANCE OF SUPER--

NO...WHAT'S HAPPENING? I'M *FLOATING?* AM I *FLOATING* NOW?

OH NO!

GAHHH!
K-RASH!
K-SHASH!

WHHHAAAAAA--!
SSKSSH!
OHMIGOSHOHMIGOSHOHMIGOSH
SSKSSH!
--AAAAAAHHHHHH!!!

BLURGLE!
BLURG!!!

PLUH!
GUH!
ZEEEEET!

--AAAAAAA
--AAAAAAAAAAAAA--
--AAAAAAA
SIGH

OKAY. OKAY, I'M FLYING. I CAN DO THIS. I CAN FLY... UNDER... CONTROL...
OH NO
LOOK OUT, OLD-TIMEY AIRPLANE!!
DOINK!
UT

OW-
OOF-
WHY?
IUSTITIA OBTINET
ENOUGH!
I DON'T WANT THIS!
I DON'T *WANT* TO BE A SUPER-HERO!
I DON'T WANT TO BE *SUPERNOVA*!!!
TZRACKATHOOM!

GUHHHH
--OH.

--I'M
ME AGAIN!
I'M NORMAL!
I'M--
FALLING?!
GAAAHHHHHH!

I TAKE IT BACK I TAKE IT BACK *I TAKE IT BACK*

IUSTITIA OBTINET

OW.

UGH.

SIGH

THIS IS THE WEIRDEST DAY EVER!

I'M AFRAID, DEAR SUPERNOVA, THAT IT IS ABOUT TO GET FAR STRANGER.

CAT?
YES...IT IS I. THE ***CAT.*** AND WE MUST SPEAK AT ONCE!
ARE YOU READY...TO LEARN OF YOUR ***DESTINY?!***

LISTEN TO ME, CHILD, THERE IS A GRAVE DANGER--

NOPE.

THE CITY IS IN *PERIL--*

NOPE.

ONLY ***YOU*** CAN STOP THE ONCOMING STORM--

NOPE NOPE ***NOPE.***

I KNOW YOU THINK ME A SIMPLE FELINE...BUT UNDERSTAND: I AM NOW SO MUCH MORE!
I WITNESSED YOUR TRANSFORMATION, AND THE ENERGIES THAT BOMBARDED YOU... THEY IN TURN AFFECTED ME!
AS A RESULT, MY INTELLECT HAS GROWN A MILLION-FOLD! THE SECRETS OF REALITY UNLOCKED...MY SENSES UNFURLED!
IT WAS AS IF I HAD BEEN IN THE DARK MY ENTIRE LIFE, AND NOW MY MIND WAS FILLED WITH LIGHT!
"AND IN THAT MOMENT, THE OVERLORDS SPOKE!
"THEY ENTERED MY MIND--THEY TASKED ME WITH ENSURING YOUR TRAINING! HELPING YOU ADJUST TO YOUR NEW EXISTENCE!
"I BECAME THEIR HERALD! THEIR VOICE! I BECAME A BEING FILLED WITH PURPOSE AND ENERGY!"

I AM **NO LONGER** JUST A HOUSE CAT! I AM **ONE WITH TIME AND SPACE!** I AM A FELINE **REBORN!**
I AM **MISTER McKITTENS!** AND I...AM YOUR **MENTOR!**

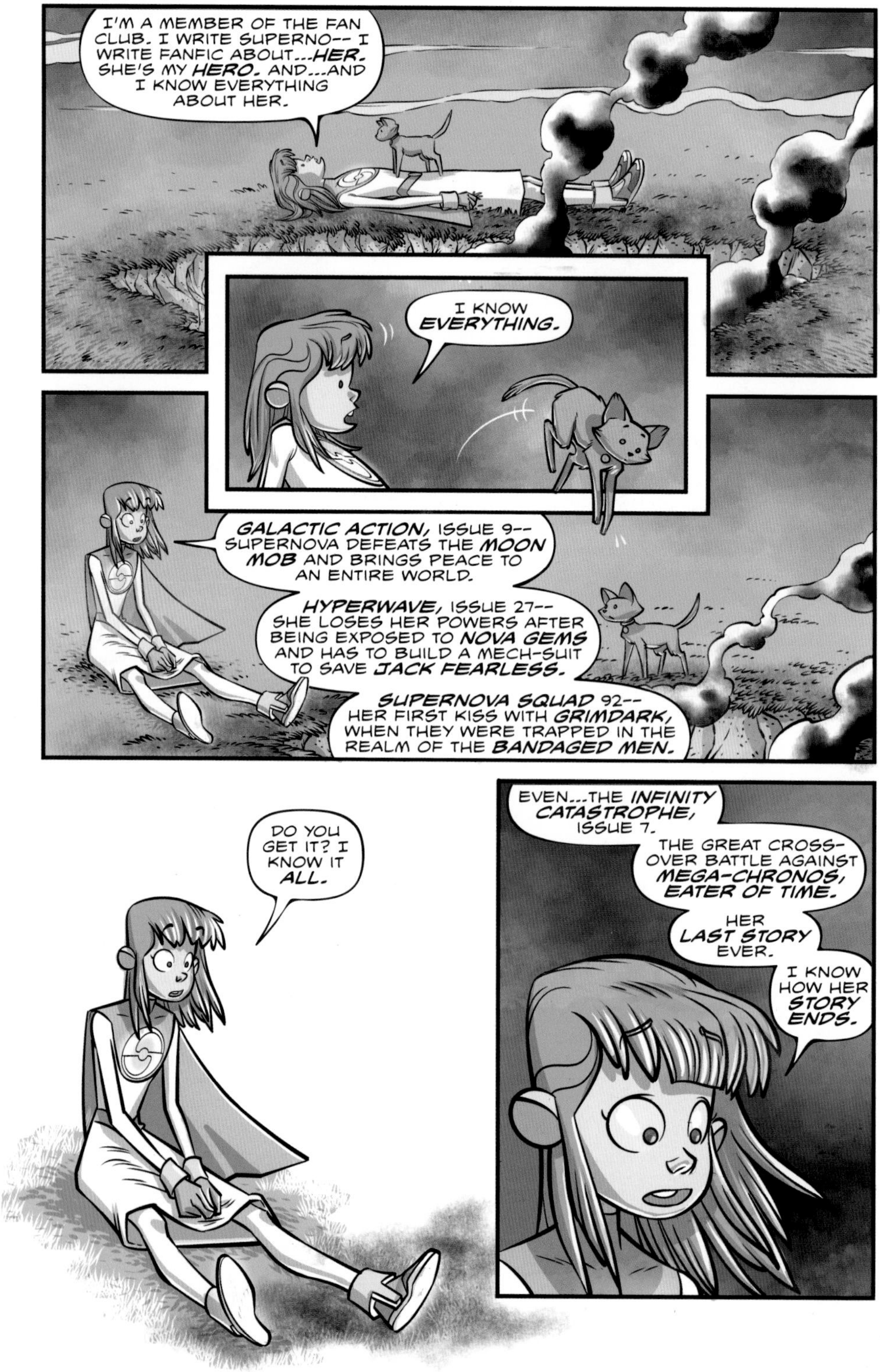

I'M A MEMBER OF THE FAN CLUB. I WRITE SUPERNO-- I WRITE FANFIC ABOUT...HER. SHE'S MY HERO. AND...AND I KNOW EVERYTHING ABOUT HER.
I KNOW EVERYTHING.
GALACTIC ACTION, ISSUE 9-- SUPERNOVA DEFEATS THE MOON MOB AND BRINGS PEACE TO AN ENTIRE WORLD.
HYPERWAVE, ISSUE 27-- SHE LOSES HER POWERS AFTER BEING EXPOSED TO NOVA GEMS AND HAS TO BUILD A MECH-SUIT TO SAVE JACK FEARLESS.
SUPERNOVA SQUAD 92-- HER FIRST KISS WITH GRIMDARK, WHEN THEY WERE TRAPPED IN THE REALM OF THE BANDAGED MEN.
DO YOU GET IT? I KNOW IT ALL.
EVEN...THE INFINITY CATASTROPHE, ISSUE 7.
THE GREAT CROSS-OVER BATTLE AGAINST MEGA-CHRONOS, EATER OF TIME.
HER LAST STORY EVER.
I KNOW HOW HER STORY ENDS.

I *CAN'T* BE HER. I DON'T WANT TO BE...
...SUPERNOVA.
ZZRACKATHOOM!
I'M JUST *PEPPER*. PEPPER PAGE.
I'M NOT A SUPERHERO.

I'M AFRAID THAT CHOICE IS NO LONGER IN YOUR HANDS.
IT IS AS THE OVERLORDS FORETOLD.
THE DESTROYER IS HERE.

HOLY MONKEYS.
NO, MY DEAR, NO.
THERE IS NOTHING HOLY ABOUT THIS.

ALSO, THERE ARE NO MONKEYS.

NOVEL COMICS GROUP
25¢ IND.
11 NOV
SUPERNOVA!
GASP!
IT'S... YOU!
WHO IS MENDAX?

COME ON.
NO.
BUT YOU MUST.
NO.
IT'S YOUR DESTINY.
NO!

FINE. I'M LOOKING. NOPE. NO EVIL EMERGING!

OH. WAIT. THERE IT IS.

THAT'S ACTUALLY PRETTY EVIL-LOOKING.

OKAY. EYE OF CHAOS. EVIL.
IN THE COMICS... THE EVIL THREATENS EVERYTHING. THE ENTIRE UNIVERSE... HOW... HOW AM I SUPPOSED TO...
IN THE... COMICS...
OOOOHHH...
RIGHT.
NO
ANY

THE EVIL EMERGES THROUGH THE EYE, BUT IN THE ORIGINAL ORIGIN IT WAS... IT WAS AN ARMY OF MONSTERS. BUT THAT WAS BEFORE THE RETCON THAT PETER DAVID WROTE...THE ONE WHERE--

OH NO... I KNOW THIS STORY.

OHMIGOSHWHEREISIT... COME ON COME ON...
SUPERNOVA VERSUS EYE SCREAM... NO...
ECLIPSA ATTACKS... DEFINITELY NO.
GUILD OF CHAMPIONS... PARADOXIA... MONSTRO...

THIS... THIS IS IT.
THE REBOOTED ORIGIN FROM THE MID-'60S BINDER ARC...
IT'S REALLY JUST LIKE THE COMIC!
LET'S SEE, THOUGH... MAYBE NOT TOTALLY JUST LIKE IT--I MEAN, THERE WAS SUPPOSED TO BE THAT MONKEY SOMEWHERE....
NO NO NO! FOCUS! THE MONKEY ISN'T IMPORTANT!
NOVEL COMICS GROUP
OKAY. SKY SPHERE. BUT IT COULDN'T BE...
I MEAN... IT CAN'T ALL BE REAL?
CAN IT?

IF IT *IS*...

THIS COULD BE REALLY, *REALLY* BAD.
NOVEL COMICS GROUP
SUPER-NOVA!

WORSE THAN *COPPER PENNY*. WORSE THAN *UNGORILLA*. WORSE THAN *ALL* OF THEM.

PEPPER? *WHAT IS IT?* WHAT HAVE YOU *DISCOVERED?*
UM...

OKAY.

SO THE *EARLY VILLAINS* WERE MOSTLY COSTUMED CLOWNS. LIKE *JABBERWOCK*, OR *KING CONUN-DRUM*...

THAT'S ALL THERE IS FOR, LIKE, A REALLY LONG TIME.
UNTIL *THIS* ISSUE.

HIS NAME IS *MENDAX*.
MENDAX, THE DESTROYER OF WORLDS.

I'M ONLY FIFTEEN YEARS OLD. MENDAX SHATTERS PEOPLE'S BRAINS WITH THE POWER OF THOUGHT!
HE CAN CONTROL TIME AND SPACE! AND PEOPLE! AND HE WANTS TO STEAL THE STAR-FORCE!
I DON'T WANT MY BRAIN SHATTERED!

PEPPER... YOU MUST SAY THE NAME. YOU MUST SAY IT NOW.

I DON'T WANT TO.
THE SHIP IS OPENING. NO NO NO...
PEPPER... PLEASE...
IT'S... IT'S...

NO WAY.

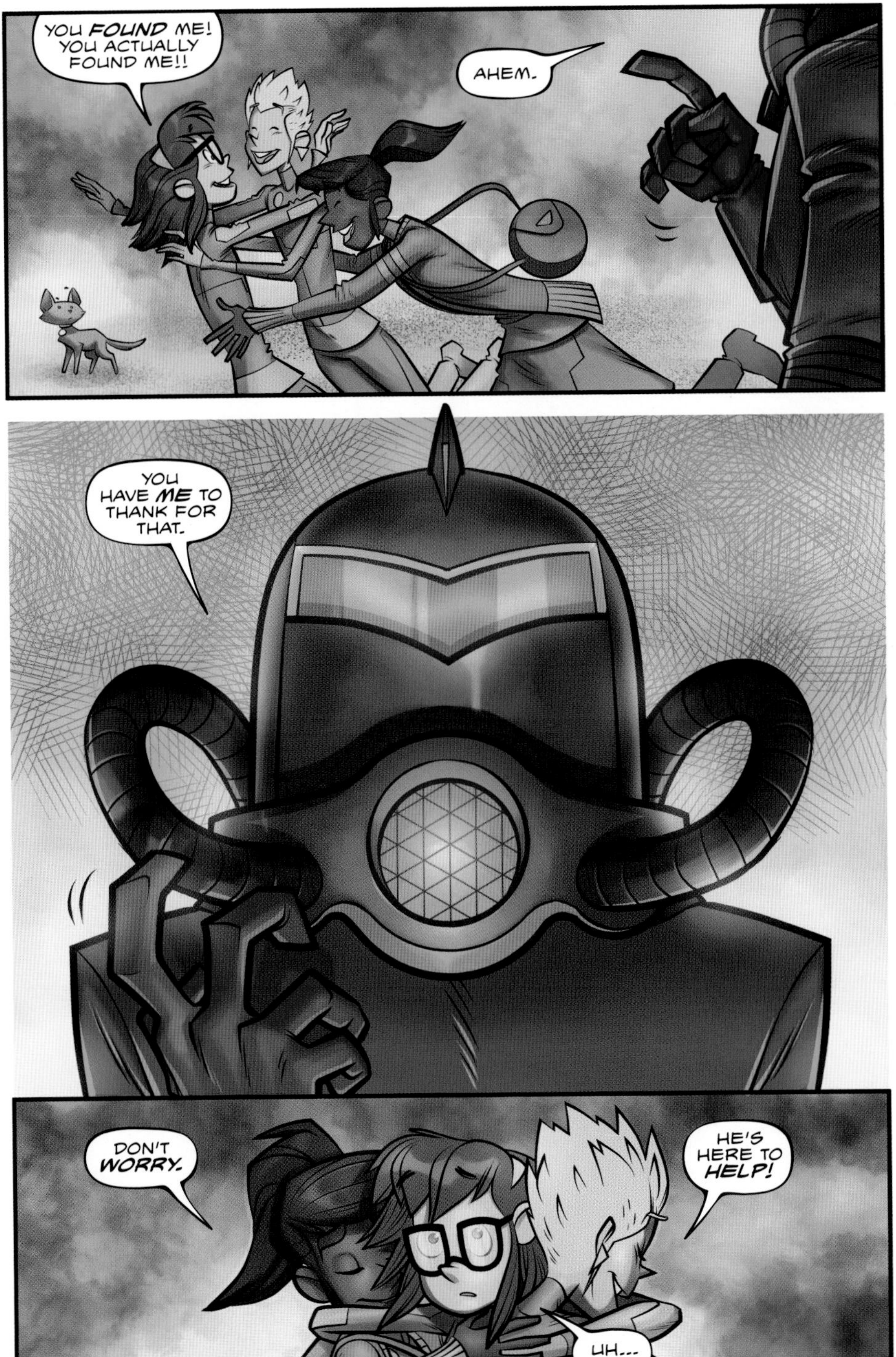

YOU HAVE ME TO THANK FOR THAT.

BUT THAT'S... THAT'S HIM. THAT'S...

PROFESSOR KILLIAN?!

BUT YOU... WHY ARE YOU DRESSED LIKE--
THIS ARMOR? A ROBOTIC SUIT DESIGNED TO HELP NAVIGATE THE TIME AND SPACE VORTEX. IT TOOK SOME TIME TO TRACK YOU DOWN, MISS PAGE.

YOU CAME TO SAVE ME? I GET TO GO HOME? FOR REAL?!

YES. OF COURSE. HOME.

DON'T WORRY!
HE'S HERE TO HELP!
UM. WHAT?

YOU ARE IN THE PRESENCE OF A DANGEROUS CREATURE, MISS PAGE. BUT DO NOT WORRY...I HAVE BROUGHT THE NECESSARY CONTAINMENT EQUIPMENT.

HSSS...!
THERE'S MY LITTLE TEST SUBJECT...

HHISSSS!

OH...YOU THOUGHT YOU COULD ESCAPE...
ROWR! RRRR!

THE RESIDUAL STARFORCE YOU'VE ABSORBED WILL BE QUITE INTERESTING TO EXAMINE...
WHOOMP
MEW?

DON'T **WORRY!**

HE'S HERE TO **HELP!**

ZOLA... TALLY...WHAT... WHAT IS **WRONG WITH YOU?**

WRONG? WITH **THEM?** NOTHING AT ALL.

I'VE SIMPLY TAUGHT THEM HOW TO **BEHAVE.**

GIRLS? GIVE PEPPER HER... **PRESENT.**

DON'T **WORRY!**

HE'S HERE TO **HELP!**

WHA--?

DO THEY?

HSSS!

HOW... INTERESTING.

ZZT!

HEY! YOU LEAVE MISTER McKITTENS ALONE!!!
DON'T WORRY!
HE'S HERE TO HELP!

MISS PAGE, I HAVE PURSUED YOU THROUGH TIME AND SPACE.
THE CAT IS NOT WHAT YOU SHOULD BE CONCERNED ABOUT RIGHT NOW.

GUHH! IT'S...THEY'RE BURNING...
SHAK!
DON'T WORRY!
WHY...WHY ARE YOU DOING THIS?!
HE'S HERE TO HELP!
PEPPER PAGE. YOU ALMOST RUINED EVERY-THING...
...YOU TOOK POSSESSION OF AN ENERGY THAT I REQUIRE.
I WAS ANGRY. BUT THEN I REALIZED...
ALL I HAD TO DO NOW TO GET THE STARFORCE...
IS RIP IT FROM A WEAK AND SIMPLE CHILD.

SUPER...
SUPERNO--
--AAAAGGGGH!!!
AH...I THOUGHT YOU MIGHT HAVE BONDED WITH THE ENERGY BY NOW. SHAPED IT WITH YOUR DELUSIONAL AND CHILDISH FLIGHTS OF FANCY.
SUPER-NOVA...
PFF.

DON'T BE A *FOOL*.
ANY ATTEMPT YOU MAKE IN ACCESSING THE *POWER WITHIN YOU*... WILL RESULT ONLY IN *PAIN*.

TALLY... ZOLA...
DON'T WORRY!

HE'S HERE TO *HELP!*

PROFESSOR KILLIAN...

YOU'RE SUPPOSED TO BE A *TEACHER!*

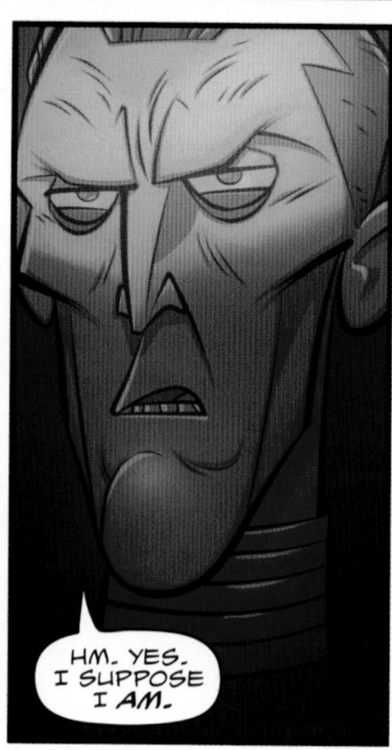
HM. YES. I SUPPOSE I *AM*.

STARFORCE DETECTED

COMMENCE EXTRACTION?

CONSIDER THIS YOUR *EDUCATION*.

FOR YEARS I SERVED THE PEOPLE. I *TOILED AWAY* TO BRING *ENLIGHTENMENT* AND *EDIFICATION* TO THE SIMPLE AND HOPELESS.

HELPING OTHERS... I HAVE LEARNED THE HARD WAY...

IT IS AN ***ABSOLUTE WASTE*** OF RESOURCES.

THAT'S...IS THAT A GOLDEN AGE COPY OF STARSTRUCK COMICS 37?!

THAT'S THE ORIGINAL ORIGIN...BEFORE THEY REVISED IT. EVEN I DON'T HAVE A COPY OF THAT BOOK!
ONLY FOUR COPIES OF THOSE SURVIVED THE GOLDEN AGE! WHERE DID YOU GET THAT?!

IT HARDLY MATTERS.
BUT THAT'S THE RAREST BOOK EVER! IT HAS THE VERY FIRST APPEARANCE OF SUP--

GYAAHHHHH!

YES.
"SUPERNOVA."

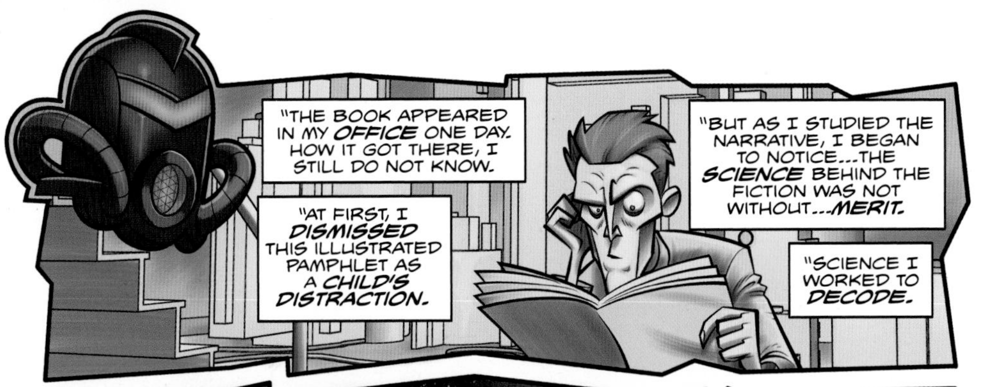
"THE BOOK APPEARED IN MY OFFICE ONE DAY. HOW IT GOT THERE, I STILL DO NOT KNOW.
"AT FIRST, I DISMISSED THIS ILLUSTRATED PAMPHLET AS A CHILD'S DISTRACTION.
"BUT AS I STUDIED THE NARRATIVE, I BEGAN TO NOTICE...THE SCIENCE BEHIND THE FICTION WAS NOT WITHOUT...MERIT.
"SCIENCE I WORKED TO DECODE.

"UNTIL...
"IT WAS AS IF A VOICE CALLED OUT ACROSS TIME AND SPACE. IT SPOKE TO ME...
"MY MIND HAD BEEN SO LIMITED BEFORE. AND THEN IT WAS LIKE A VOID OPENED UP, AND INFORMATION POURED INTO ME.
"I KNEW IN THAT MOMENT...THE STARFORCE WAS REAL, AND I COULD FOLLOW THE INSTRUCTIONS LAID OUT IN THIS COMIC BOOK AND CAPTURE IT FOR MY OWN.

"WHEN I DISCOVERED YOUR AFFINITY FOR THE CHARACTER, I BELIEVED I MIGHT BE ABLE TO PEEL FURTHER BITS OF INFORMATION FROM YOUR WEAK, MALLEABLE BRAIN.
"I WAS SO CLOSE TO CLAIMING THE POWER. MY MACHINE WAS ALMOST READY..."

...BUT THEN YOU STOLE IT FROM ME!

YOU WERE USING YOUR STUPID MACHINE ON A CAT!
YOU FOOLISH CHILD. HOW LITTLE YOU UNDERSTAND.

IT DOESN'T MATTER...YOU MUST FORSAKE THE POWER THAT IS RIGHTFULLY MINE. I ALONE POSSESS THE INTELLECT TO WIELD IT.
IT WAS PROMISED TO ME!

I DIDN'T EVEN WANT IT! JUST...LET MY FRIENDS GO FIRST. TAKE WHATEVER YOU WANT...BUT YOU HAVE TO LET THEM GO!
EXTRACTION AT 100%
SYSTEM READY!!!

HM...

I WILL NOT.

SUP... SUPER...
AAAAAHH!

STOP IT! PLEASE!

THE ENERGY...I CAN FEEL IT SURGING INTO ME!
SO MUCH POWER! GREATER THAN THAT OF AN EXPLODING SUN!
WHO WOULD HAVE THOUGHT A PITIFUL, TIMID, TEENAGE NOBODY MIGHT HARNESS IT!

IMAGINE WHAT I WILL BE ABLE TO DO...
WITH THE STARFORCE, I COULD END WARS. I COULD ELEVATE HUMANITY... REMOLD IT!

I WILL CLEANSE THE UNIVERSE OF THE UNWORTHY! ONLY THE TRULY BRILLIANT WILL REMAIN!

THE COSMIC ENERGIES CALL TO ME! THEIR VOICES GROW LOUDER AND LOUDER! AND MY MIND...I CAN SEE MORE AND MORE OF WHAT THE UNIVERSE HAS TO OFFER ME!
A TEACHER... TO THINK I WASTED MY LIFE AS A MERE TEACHER!
NO!!
DON'T WORRY!
HE'S HERE TO HELP!
STOP! PLEASE STOP!!
THE POWER IS MINE! THE POWER OF THE GODS! THE POWER OF...

...SUPERNOVA!
AAH!
I SUPPOSE I SHOULD THANK YOU, PEPPER PAGE...
YOUR INCOMPETENCE MADE MY ASCENSION POSSIBLE AFTER ALL!
NO...NO, THIS ISN'T HOW THE STORY...
PLEASE... SOMEONE...
SOMEONE HELP ME.
SUPERNOVA
PATHETIC.
YOU SQUANDERED YOUR CHANCE TO LIVE OUT YOUR FOOLISH FANTASIES.
BUT DON'T WORRY...
YOU WON'T REGRET IT FOR LONG...
SUPERNOVA
WHAT...? YOUR VOICE...YOU'RE FADING...I CAN HEAR...

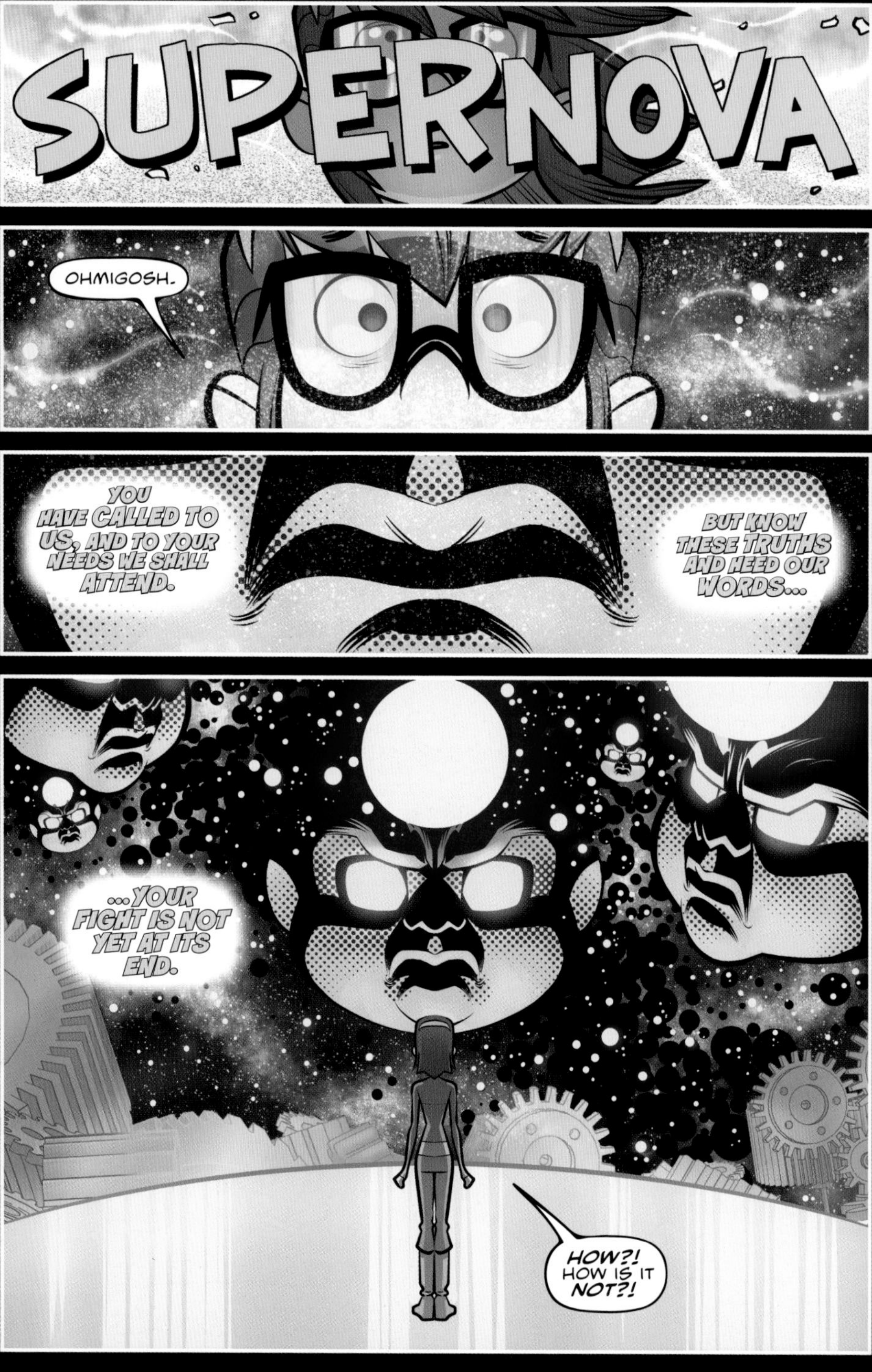

OHMIGOSH.

BUT KNOW THESE TRUTHS AND HEED OUR WORDS...

...YOUR FIGHT IS NOT YET AT ITS END.

HOW?! HOW IS IT NOT?!

HOW AM I SUPPOSED TO DEAL WITH THIS?! I'M... I'M JUST A KID!

I'M NOT HER. I'M NOT A SUPERHERO! AND EVEN IF I WAS...

IT'S ALL GONE... HE TOOK IT!

I'M NOT SUPER.
I'M NOT IMPORTANT.
I'M NOT ANYTHING.

ZOLA AND TALLY...THEY NEED HELP! PLEASE! AND...AND...
I'M NOT STRONG ENOUGH! I'M NOT...NOT BRAVE ENOUGH! IT'S TOO MUCH!
PLEASE.
YOU PICKED THE WRONG PERSON.
I'M... SCARED.
YOUR FEAR IS GOOD, CHILD. YOUR DREAD, AS WELL.
THEY BRING WITH THEM YOUR COURAGE AND DARING.
YOU HAVE ALWAYS BEEN SUPERNOVA.
YOU EMERGE AS THE DARKNESS IS FLARING.
WE DID NOT CHOOSE YOU, SUPERNOVA. FOR THAT IS WHO YOU ARE.
IT IS THE ONLY PATH YOU WILL EVER SEE. YOU ARE ONE WITH THE QUORUM OF STARS.

YOUR FATE IS UNCHANGING, YOUR FUTURE YOUR BURDEN.

FOREVER ITS OUTCOME YOU'LL KNOW.

BUT IT IS YOUR CHOICE...

...WILL FEAR SHEPHERD YOUR JOURNEY?

OR WILL YOU ARISE...

...A HERO?

YOU HEAR, MISS PAGE? YOU THINK YOU'RE SOME KIND OF HERO?
BAH! EVEN NOW, YOUR MIND IS A MILLION MILES AWAY!

IT DOESN'T MATTER...
YOU'VE SERVED YOUR PURPOSE, AS HAVE YOUR FRIENDS.

...A HERO.

THE POWER I RIGHTFULLY DESERVE IS FINALLY MINE!
AND WITH IT... THE GATEWAY TO ETERNITY WILL BE OPENED!

NO MORE, PROFESSOR.
NO.
YOU CAN'T TAKE THIS POWER!
'CAUSE IT'S NOT JUST THE STARFORCE.
THE POWER IS ME.

SUPER

GUH.

I'M **NOT** GOING TO GIVE UP, KILLIAN. **NOT EVER.**

BECAUSE I DON'T FIGHT FOR **MYSELF...**

...I FIGHT FOR WHAT IS *RIGHT.*
YOU'RE *NOTHING!* JUST A *NOBODY!*
AND I WILL *DESTROY* YOU!
WHA?
URK!

DON'T WORRY.
HE'S HERE TO HELP.
I DON'T KNOW HOW YOU ACCESSED THE STARFORCE...
BUT I PROMISE YOU, THESE CHILDISH HEROICS END NOW. THERE'S NO WAY YOU CAN MATCH THE POWER OF MY INTELLECT!
IT'S OVER, PROFESSOR. I'M NOT GOING TO LET YOU BULLY ME.
I'M A HERO.

ZORK!
AND NOTHING YOU DO CAN CHANGE THAT!
TOSS!
BOOM!

WHAM!
ZEEEEET!
POW!
ZARK!

NO...
IT'S NOT POSSIBLE...
KLOOM!

DON'T WORRY!
...WHA?
HE'S HERE TO HELP!
NO...
SNAP OUT OF IT! KILLIAN'S CONTROLLING YOU!
ERG...
LISTEN! I'M WINNING NOW...BUT I CAN FEEL HIS POWER GROWING!
YOU HAVE TO LET ME GO BEFORE IT'S TOO LATE!
HMM...

YOU FOOL. I TOLD YOU...HH...YOU CAN'T DEFEAT ME.

YOU MAY HAVE USURPED THE STARFORCE, BUT YOUR FRIENDS' FRAGILE LITTLE MINDS ARE UNDER THE POWER OF MY MACHINES!

THOUGH NOW...WITH THE NEW POWERS I HAVE...
...PERHAPS I WILL FEED ON THEIR MINDS DIRECTLY!
HEHHEH HAHAHAH!

YES...IMAGINE THE FEAST! ALL THE WORLD'S THOUGHTS, EMPOWERING ME...
I WOULD BE LIKE A GOD!

GLK!
BLURG!

WHAT--?
THERE'S **NO WAY** YOU COULD HAVE **DEPROGRAMMED** THEM WITHOUT ACCESS TO MY **SHIP! HOW--?**
THAT CAT! IT MUST BE **HIM!**
NO MATTER. SOON I WILL **RETURN HIM** TO MY OPERATING--

KLIK

EH?

THE *TIME PORTAL?* OPENING? BUT WHY--

NOW, SUPERNOVA! BEFORE IT'S TOO LATE!

OH NO.

NO. NO! *NO!!* I WON'T GO BACK! I'LL FEED ON YOUR MIND! THE STARFORCE WILL BE--
POW!

CUUUUURRRRSEEE YOOOOUUUUUUU!!!!!

OHMIGOSH.

I REALLY *DID IT.*

I REALLY AM A *SUPERHERO!*

I REALLY AM SUPERNOVA!
SHRACKOOM!

EVERYTHING THE OVERLORDS OF ORDER SAID--IT WAS TRUE.
THE POWER IS ME.
IT'S ALWAYS BEEN ME.

PEPPER...?

YOU'RE OKAY!
DID ALL THAT REALLY JUST HAPPEN? IT'S SO FOGGY...
PEPPER, YOU'RE A SUPERHERO??!!

I KNOW! IT'S TOTALLY BONKERS!
I'M JUST GLAD YOU'RE OKAY! WHEN YOU VANISHED--
CHANGE BACK AND LET ME TAKE HOLOS! IT'S SO FREAKING COOL!!!

I'M SO SORRY ABOUT KILLIAN AND EVERYTHING!
IT HAPPENED SO FAST! YOU GOT TRAPPED AND THEN HE ZAPPED US WITH SOME MACHINE--
WILL IT WORK IF I SAY IT, TOO? "SUPERNOVA!" "SUPERNOVA!"
AHEM.

HUMAN CHILDREN, I AM LOATH TO INTERRUPT THIS JOYOUS REUNION, BUT THERE IS A PRESSING MATTER TO ADDRESS.

WHAT IS IT, MCKITTENS?
YOU MEAN THE CAT? THE CAT CAN TALK?
NOT THE WEIRDEST THING TODAY, TALLY!

KILLIAN RUPTURED TIME AND SPACE TO TRANSPORT HIMSELF HERE.
THE GOOD NEWS IS THAT THIS HOLE WILL REPAIR ITSELF RATHER THAN CONSUME ALL OF REALITY.
THE BAD NEWS IS THAT IT IS REPAIRING ITSELF RATHER... QUICKLY.
SO THAT MEANS...
THE ONLY WAY BACK TO YOUR ORIGINAL TIMELINE IS THROUGH THAT PORTAL. AND I'M AFRAID THERE IS ONE MORE THING...
AS UNSTABLE AS IT HAS BECOME, IT WILL REQUIRE AN OUTSIDE ENERGY SOURCE TO KEEP IT FROM COLLAPSING DURING TRANSIT.
A POWER THAT REMAINS ON THIS SIDE OF THE TIME PORTAL.
...
YOU MEAN... YOU MEAN ME.
I'M THE ONLY ONE WHO CAN GENERATE THAT KIND OF POWER.
YOU MEAN I CAN'T GO BACK.

I THINK I FINALLY KNOW WHERE I BELONG.

I'M SUPERNOVA.

ZOLA, TALLY...I'M ALL RIGHT.
I DON'T THINK I'VE EVER FELT THIS ALL RIGHT BEFORE.
I'M HAPPY.

BUT...YOU'RE OUR BEST FRIEND.
WE'LL MISS YOU.
YOU'LL SEE ME AGAIN. SOON. I KNOW THE COMICS, AND I GET TO TRAVEL IN TIME...A LOT.
THIS ISN'T THE END.

LADIES, THE PORTAL MUST CLOSE SOON. IF IT DOES NOT...THE CONSEQUENCES COULD BE DISASTROUS.

HEY... IT'S OKAY.
I'M NOT RUNNING AWAY FROM ANYTHING THIS TIME.

I THINK I'M ACTUALLY RUNNING TOWARD SOMETHING.

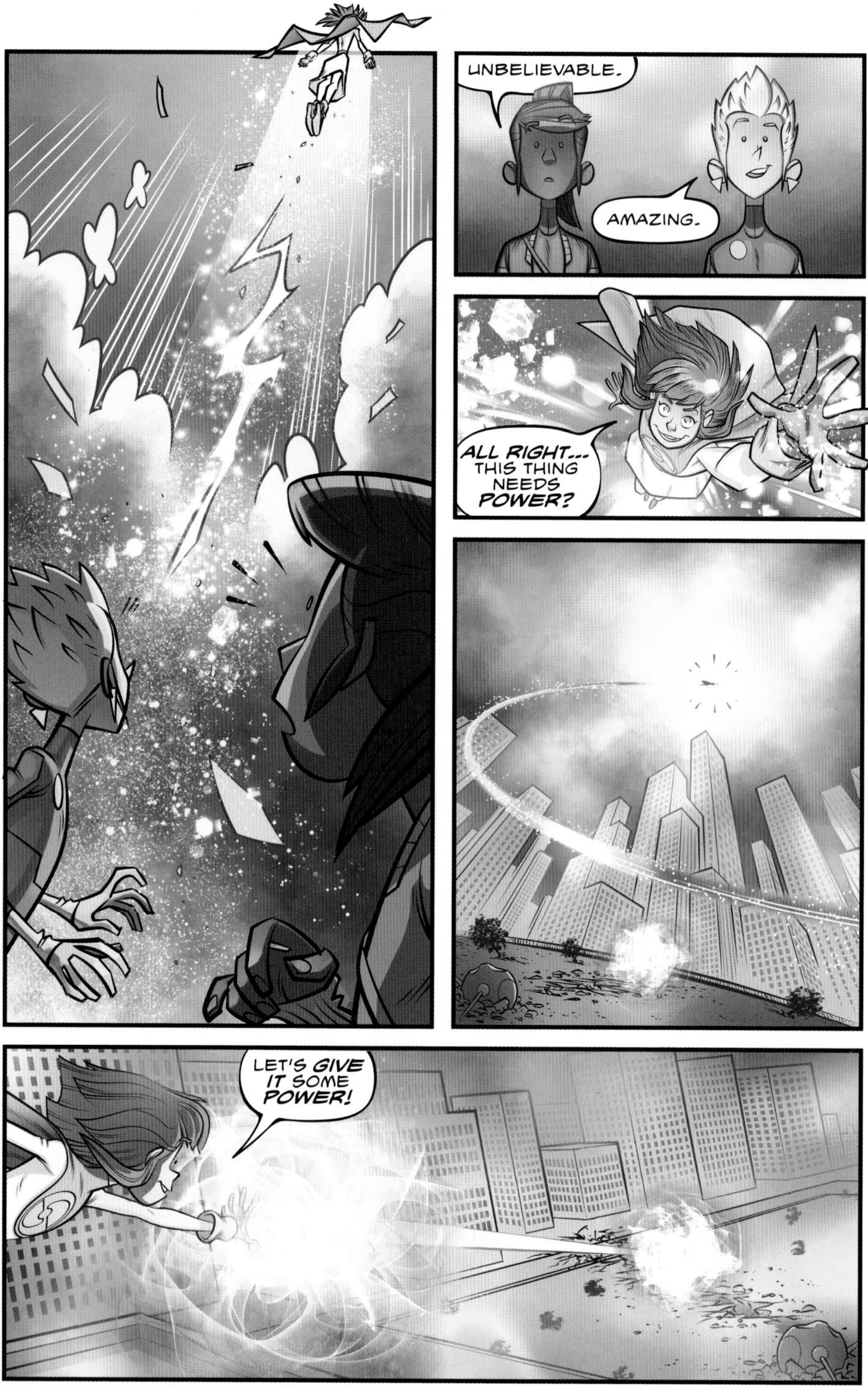

UNBELIEVABLE.
AMAZING.

ALL RIGHT... THIS THING NEEDS POWER?

LET'S GIVE IT SOME POWER!

SHE'S DOING IT! IT'S STABILIZING!

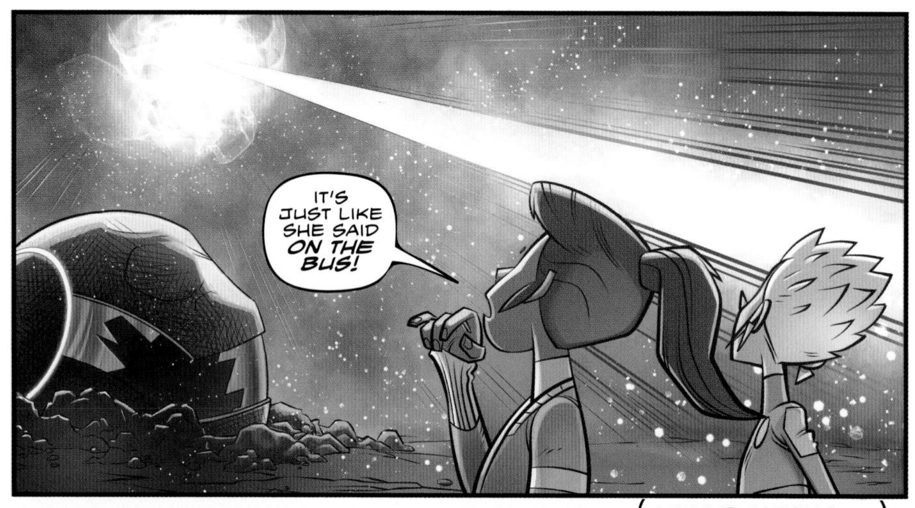
IT'S JUST LIKE SHE SAID ON THE BUS!

SHE'S PUNCHING IT... WITH RAINBOWS.
AND IT'S AWESOME.

IT'S READY! GO, CHILDREN! HURRY, BEFORE IT'S TOO LATE!

COME ON.

ONE MORE ADVENTURE!

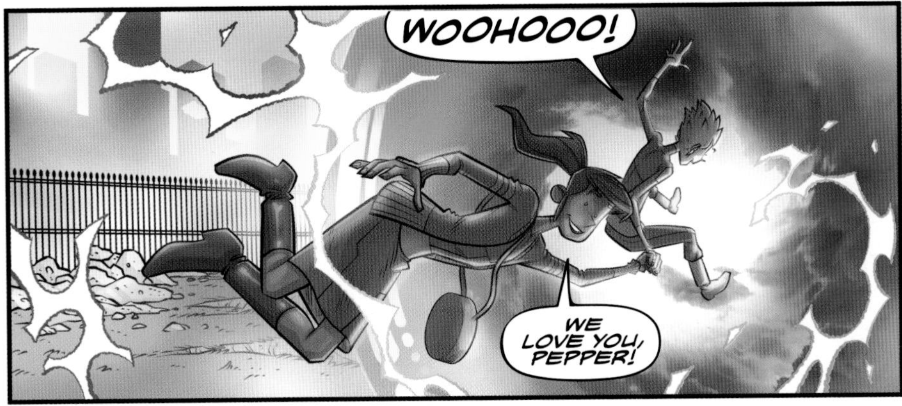
WOOHOOO!
WE LOVE YOU, PEPPER!

IT'S GOING TO ***WHAT*** NOW?

SHOOM

OH NO!

SUPERNOVA?

THE GATEWAY...IT'S *CLOSED!* ARE YOU...?
McKITTENS...?

PEPPER?

AND SO ***STERLING CITY*** WAS SAVED...

THE PEOPLE OF THE CITY HAD WITNESSED ***WONDERS*** THAT CANNOT BE UNSEEN...

THEY SAW ***EVIL*** RIP THE SKY APART, AND THEY SAW A YOUNG GIRL ***RISK EVERYTHING*** TO PUT IT BACK TOGETHER.

THEY SAW *SUPERNOVA*.
A HERO OF *HOPE, COMPASSION, AND LIBERTY*.
AND IT LEFT THEM...

...*INSPIRED*.
IUSTITIA OBTINET
IN THE MONTHS SINCE THE BATTLE, *STATUES* HAVE BEEN ERECTED. *POEMS* AND *SONGS* WRITTEN. *STORIES* TOLD.

ALL IN HONOR OF THE BEING THAT APPEARED FROM NOWHERE TO *SAVE HUMANITY*.
WAIT WAIT *WAIT!*
BUT THEY GOT *EVERYTHING WRONG!*
COMIC RELIEF
COMIC RELIEF

ACTION FIGURE!
ACTION FIGURE!
ACTION FIGURE!
THE AMAZING ORIGIN OF THE STUPENDOUS SUPERNOVA
SUPERNOVA POSTERS $10
BUTTONS 99¢
THE EVIL FROM THE PORTAL WASN'T A BUNCH OF SUPER-VILLAINS! AND MENDAX NEVER REALLY SHOWED UP!

AND THEY DREW ME LIKE AN ADULT! UGH! WHAT IS WRONG WITH COMICS ARTISTS!
Hey Kids!
GET THESE PRIZES
TALES TO LEAVE YOU STARSTRUCK

THIS IS HER VERY FIRST APPEARANCE, AND IT'S TOTALLY OFF-CANON ALREADY!
COMIC RELIEF
NEW COMICS THIS WEEK

GETTING THE DETAILS RIGHT SHOULDN'T BE SO HARD! I MEAN, THE ENTIRE CITY SAW THE FIGHT!
WHY DO WRITERS ALWAYS HAVE TO MAKE STUFF UP RATHER THAN JUST TELL A GOOD STORY?
THIS IS WHY YOU GET ALL THOSE REBOOTS...
COMIC RELIEF
#1 RECORDS
AND SO, THE ORIGIN STORY OF SUPERNOVA HAS COME TO AN END.

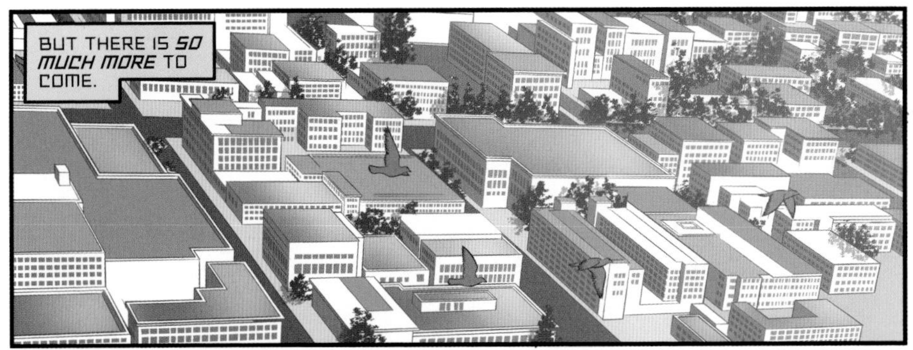
BUT THERE IS SO MUCH MORE TO COME.

HEROIC ALLIES... SINISTER ENEMIES...

ADVENTURE... INTRIGUE... DANGER.
STERLING HIGH SCHOOL

ALREADY IN THESE LAST FEW MONTHS, PEPPER HAS MADE GREAT STRIDES IN HER ROLE AS SUPERNOVA.
STERLING HIGH SCHOOL

A WEEK AFTER KILLIAN'S SHIP WAS DESTROYED, SUPERNOVA DEFEATED THE ICY EVIL OF THE CORRUPT CRIMINAL CALLED EYE SCREAM.
★ GO STERLING STARS! ★
DRAMA CLUB TRYOUTS

A WEEK AFTER THAT, SHE UNCOVERED THE MALEVOLENT UNDERTAKINGS OF THE MASTER MAGICIAN KNOWN AS HYPNOTICA.

THE TOY BRIGADE WAS BROKEN. KING CONUNDRUM'S PUZZLES WERE ALL SOLVED. THE MUFFIN MAN'S CRIME KITCHEN CLOSED.
23
24
25
ORDER BALANCED AGAINST CHAOS. JUST AS THE OVERLORDS WANTED.

BUT IN THE SPIRIT OF BALANCE... A SUPER-HERO IS NOT THE ONLY THING THAT PEPPER PAGE SHOULD BE.
23
AND SO WE ARE HERE...
PEPPER NICKNAMED IT "THE LOCKER OF SOLACE."

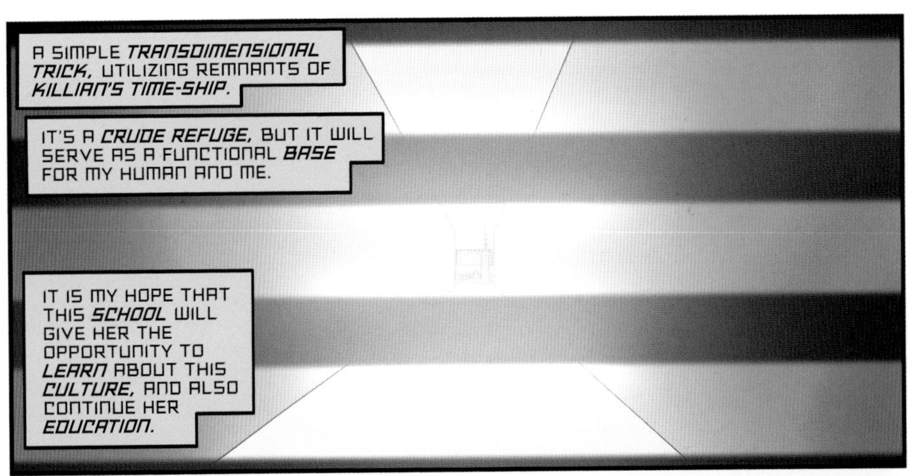
A SIMPLE *TRANSDIMENSIONAL TRICK,* UTILIZING REMNANTS OF *KILLIAN'S TIME-SHIP.*
IT'S A *CRUDE REFUGE,* BUT IT WILL SERVE AS A FUNCTIONAL *BASE* FOR MY HUMAN AND ME.
IT IS MY HOPE THAT THIS *SCHOOL* WILL GIVE HER THE OPPORTUNITY TO *LEARN* ABOUT THIS *CULTURE,* AND ALSO CONTINUE HER *EDUCATION.*

A PLACE WHERE SHE CAN FIND THE *BALANCE* BETWEEN SUPERHERO AND TEENAGE GIRL.
A PLACE WHERE SHE CAN *BUILD NEW FRIENDSHIPS.*

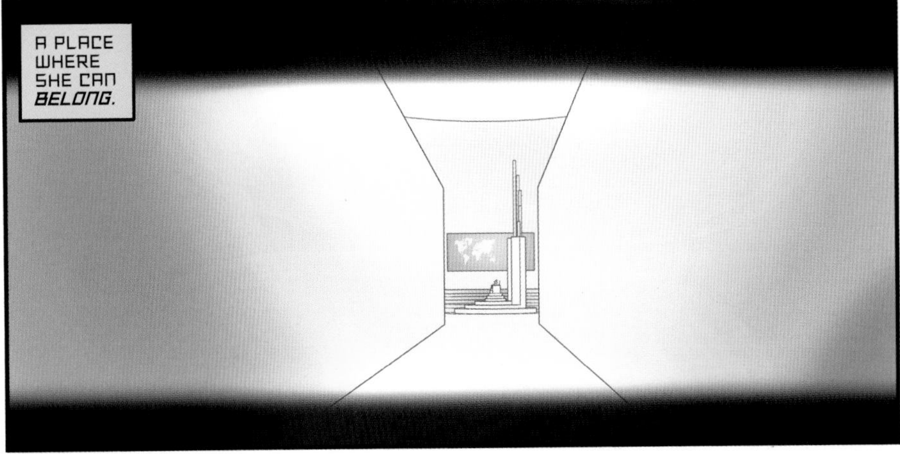
A PLACE WHERE SHE CAN *BELONG.*

OF THE *PROFESSOR*, THERE IS *NO SIGN*. THE *EVIL* THAT EMPOWERED HIM APPEARS TO HAVE BEEN *REMOVED FROM THIS REALITY*.

BUT THE *COMIC BOOKS* PEPPER CARRIED THROUGH THE TIME STREAM PROMISE *ONE THING*...

...THERE WILL *ALWAYS* BE A NEED FOR A *HERO*.

PEPPER BELIEVES THAT THESE PULP-PRINTED STORIES THAT SHE HAS COLLECTED WILL SERVE HER AS A MAP TO HER OWN FUTURE.
I MAY BE BUT A SIMPLE CAT, ALBEIT ONE GIFTED WITH COSMIC POWER BEYOND RECKONING...

...BUT I THINK THAT FATE IS A CURIOUS AND DECEPTIVE THING.

AND THAT THE TRUE SCOPE OF AN ADVENTURE MUST BE LIVED...IT CANNOT BE CONTAINED TO PANELS AND PAGES AND DRAWINGS.
LIFE IS MEANT TO BE LIVED; THE PATHS UNCOVERED AS YOU GO.

AND IN THE CURIOUS STORY OF PEPPER PAGE...

...I TRULY BELIEVE *ANYTHING MIGHT BE POSSIBLE.*

THE END

SUPERNOVA!
GALLERY
WELCOME TO THE SUPERNOVA GALLERY!
AN EXCLUSIVE LOOK AT THE MAKING OF THE INFINITE ADVENTURES OF SUPERNOVA!

COMICS ARE A LOT OF WORK TO MAKE.
EVERYTHING IS DRAWN BY HAND, AND EVERY DECISION IS SUPER IMPORTANT!
I MEAN, THE ARTIST TRIED OUT MORE THAN FIFTY COLOR DESIGNS FOR MY COSTUME ALONE!
THAT'S BONKERS!

AND LOOK AT ALL THESE *COMIC BOOK COVERS!*
THE ARTIST MADE A *TON* OF ART THAT YOU BARELY EVEN SEE IN THE *STORY!*
BUT I LIKE IT BECAUSE IT MAKES THE WORLD OF *SUPERNOVA* SEEM *SO REAL!*

12¢
TALES TO LEAVE YOU
STARSTRUCK
THE SUPERNOVA SAGA BEGINS HERE!

SUPER-NOVA
NOVEL COMICS GROUP
25¢ 71 JULY 02455
SUPER-NOVA!
WHO IS IT?!
WHAT IS IT?!
WHEN DID IT COME FROM?!

SUPER-NOVA
NOVEL COMICS GROUP
25¢ 71 JULY 02455
SUPER-NOVA!
BEHOLD! THE UNIVERSE'S GREATEST FOE:
DARK ULTRANOVA!

SUPER-
NOVA
NOVEL COMICS GROUP
25¢
93
JAN
02453
SUPERNOVA!
IN THE CLUTCHES OF
ECLIPSA!

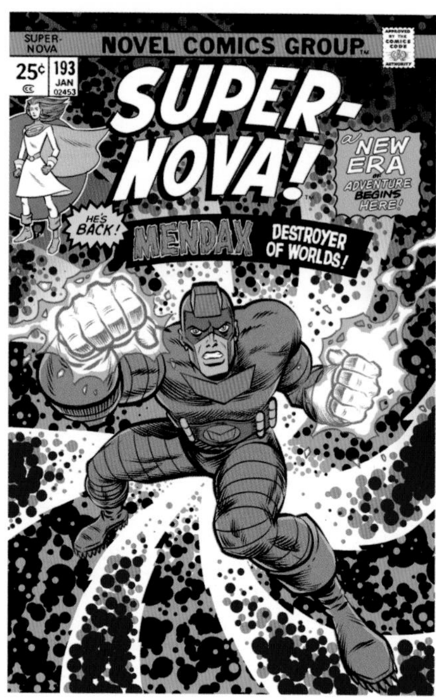
SUPER-
NOVA
NOVEL COMICS GROUP
25¢
193
JAN
02453
SUPER-
NOVA!
a NEW ERA ADVENTURE BEGINS HERE!
HE'S BACK!
MENDAX
DESTROYER OF WORLDS!

SUPERNOVA!
#1
64 PAGES OF COMICS
ALL IN GOOD FUN
THE AMAZING ORIGIN OF
THE STUPENDOUS
SUPERNOVA

SUPERNOVA!
NOVEL COMICS GROUP
25¢
IND.
11
NOV
GASP!
IT'S... YOU!
WHO IS
MENDAX?

AFTER A SCRIPT IS WRITTEN, THE ***ARTIST*** USUALLY SKETCHES OUT A BUNCH OF ***DESIGNS*** TO GET A FEEL FOR THE ***CHARACTER*** AND THE ***WORLD*** THEY LIVE IN.
SCHOOL BUS
SKETCHES ARE ***PRETTY COOL***, BUT I PREFER TO BE FULLY ***INKED AND COLORED!***

EXPLORE NEW WORLDS WITH :01

First Second
firstsecondbooks.com

The Creepy Case Files of Margo Maloo
by Drew Weing
"Smart, spooky mystery."
—*Booklist*

Cucumber Quest
by Gigi D.G.
"Candy-colored charmer."
—*Kirkus*

The Time Museum
by Matthew Loux
★ "Fresh, fast, and funny."
—*Kirkus*, starred review

Star Scouts
by Mike Lawrence
★ "Brilliant worldbuilding."
—*Kirkus*, starred review

The Nameless City
by Faith Erin Hicks
"Breathtaking."
—*New York Times*

Astronaut Academy
by Dave Roman
"Involved and complex comedy."
—*Booklist*

Robot Dreams
by Sara Varon
★ "Tender, funny, and wise."
—*Publishers Weekly*, starred review

Giants Beware!
by Jorge Aguirre and Rafael Rosado
"Rollicking fun story."
—*New York Times*

The Unsinkable Walker Bean
by Aaron Renier
★ "Rip-roaring adventure."
—*Booklist*, starred review

Zita the Spacegirl
by Ben Hatke
"Adventurous, exciting, funny, and moving."
—*ICv2*

Battling Boy
by Paul Pope
"Dazzling."
—*New York Times*

Mighty Jack
by Ben Hatke
★ "Very mighty indeed."
—*Kirkus*, starred review

The Dam Keeper
by Robert Kondo and Dice Tsutsumi
"Profound and touching."
—*Paste*

Animus
by Antoine Revoy
"Bewildering and unnerving."
—*Kirkus*

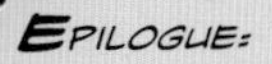
EPILOGUE:

IUSTITIA
OBTINET

...THE END?

FOR STEVE B, WHO HAS ALWAYS BEEN THERE FOR US, AND DANNY ADAMS, WHO WAS LIKE A FATHER TO ME AND WILL BE MISSED —LQW

FOR ERIN, WHO MAKES ME BELIEVE IN SUPERHEROES MORE EVERY DAY —EMJ

Published by First Second
First Second is an imprint of Roaring Brook Press,
a division of Holtzbrinck Publishing Holdings Limited Partnership
120 Broadway, New York, NY 10271
firstsecondbooks.com
mackids.com

Library of Congress Control Number: 2020911248

First edition, 2021
Edited by Calista Brill and Steve Behling
Cover and interior book design by Sunny Lee
Printed in China by Toppan Leefung Printing Ltd., Dongguan City, Guangdong Province

The book is penciled with a vintage 1950s Wearever brand mechanical pencil on
20# Hammermill Copy Plus 8.5" x 11" copy paper, and the final art is digitally inked and
painted in Clip Studio Paint and Photoshop.

ISBN 978-1-250-21692-2 (paperback)
1 3 5 7 9 10 8 6 4 2

ISBN 978-1-250-21691-5 (hardcover)
1 3 5 7 9 10 8 6 4 2